SWEET AND DEADLY

The jolly girl with the sweet face stood staring at him in open-mouthed wonder. Her lime-green dress had been caught back against her thighs, and she really did look nice. He let the electronic circuits slide the gun back up under his sleeve.

From the doorway to the cabin where the girl paused stepped the blocky Frifman. His face showed controlled power now, directed to anger and decision.

In the infinitesimal instant that Hook knew he had blundered, that he should not have let the gun slip back, the Krifman fired. A blossoming cloud of nothingness overtook Ryder Hook in the stun-gun's blast. The thing was set to full-power and Ryder Hook's consciousness, despite that skull of his, vanished like a dissolving dream at dawn...

The Hook Series:

4

STAR-SPANNING
MAN OF THE FUTURE

HOOK

THE VIRILITY GENE

by Tully Zetford

PINNACLE BOOKS • **NEW YORK CITY**

HOOK: THE VIRILITY GENE

Copyright © 1975 by Tully Zetford

All rights reserved, including the right to reproduce this book or portions thereof in any form.

A Pinnacle Books edition, published by special arrangement with New English Library Limited, London.

ISBN: 0-523-00800-7

First printing, January 1976

Cover illustration by Dick Kohfield

Printed in the United States of America

PINNACLE BOOKS, INC.
275 Madison Avenue
New York, N.Y. 10016

④

**STAR-SPANNING
MAN OF THE FUTURE**

HOOK

THE VIRILITY GENE

1

Ryder Hook first heard a rumor of the so-called Virility Gene in that nastily-escalating brawl in a sleezy deep-freeze satellite orbiting a best-forgotten planet of the Enares system. Hook ducked his head out of the way of an explosive shot that splattered the bulkhead with pock marks. The controls had already been set to dump a Star-Hard's consignment of deep-frozen passengers down to the required temperature for starflight Hard. Outside the satellite's hull the stars of the galaxy were whirling away; and here in this bubble of air Ryder Hook was likely to get himself killed—and for no good purpose.

"Keep your head down, Flakey," he said to the Drossan, whose plate-fab clothes concealed an agile and eel-like body, and whose four sinuous arms curled around, severally, a cosh, a length of metalloy chain, a twenty-five centimeter knife and a Drossan prayer book.

"I just came to be frozen for the Star-Hard," said Flakey, his slit-mouth showing absolute annoyance, his eyes, wide-mounted on mobile tubes, wriggling. His neck—all one and a half meters of it—coiled down to bring his sleek head on a level with Hook's. "These gonils have no conception of courtesy."

1

"You keep your head down or they'll blow it off."

Hook's own annoyance was contained by his half-resigned, half-resentful acceptance that no one could expect to go through life in the galaxy of the hundred and first century without bumping into trouble of one kind or another. He always tried to keep out of trouble. Other people, with even less scruples than he had—and his scruples would fit on a micro-dot and leave room for the Galactic Encyclopedia—would insist on involving him in this kind of punch-up.

The fighting died for a moment, and Hook settled comfortably in the rear of an overturned computer console and took out a prepacked sandwich. He and Flakey shared it amicably. Every now and then a shot cracked out, or a dis-gel gun spurted, and sometimes there was a shout of pain or a shriek of horror at the inevitable diliquescing end.

Then Flakey, the Drossan, told Hook something of the Virility Gene. He'd heard it was to be found on a planet—whose whereabouts he did not, to his infinite regret at that time, know—and that its owners, cultivators, miners, or just plain synthesizers, kept a stranglehold on its export.

"If you believe half the things you hear among the stars about the Virility Gene, Hook," Flakey said, squirming to be comfortable. "You'd be running your tail off for parsecs."

"I don't happen to belong to a race blessed with tails."

"You don't—I hadn't noticed."

"And, Flakey, I've warned you three times. Those idiots out there are shooting at each other. I have absolutely no desire to find out about what. As soon as the planetary enforcers arrive and clear the situation up, we can get frozen Hard. The warning stands—keep your wriggly little head down!"

"You're going to Lakashimi, right, Hook?"

"Yes."

A burst of dis-gel splattered across the corner of the

console and both men hunched away. A drop of that on the skin would mean the rapid melting of the body, to leave only a puddle. And then even the puddle would vanish.

"Feller called Gaines came from Lakashimi. Funny guy."

Perhaps it was a memory of the funny guy called Gaines, who hailed from Lakashimi, that made Flakey's sinuous squirmings take his sleek and agile body too far from the computer console.

Hook, whose own dis-gel gun remained neurally and electronically affixed to his left wrist, yelled.

He should have saved his breath.

Flakey's charming head disappeared in the explosive concussion of a shot from a Swan-Durk magnum.

Smoke coiled in the freezer complex. Hook slid past the toppling still-flopping body of Flakey. He saw the Riffian who had shot Flakey, glaring about wildly, the Swan-Durk big in his fist. Hook's dis-gel leaped into his hand and he fired. The Riffian took the shot in the face, and instantly, screaming, clawed at himself. He knew he had seconds to live.

Hook watched him shrink and melt and deliquesce.

"Curd," said Ryder Hook. "Ill-mannered gonil, interrupting an interesting conversation."

That was the first time Hook had heard about the Virility Gene.

The second time Hook heard about the Virility Gene was in a lusciously decadent Palace of FU Delights, on Sonleary, over in the out-of-the-way Usica Cluster. Although Hook did not care much for the overblown and much-vaunted charms of Shashmeeri dancing girls, all long white legs and impossibly pneumatic breasts and bulbous hips, he had to concede that the girl dancing now was a real artist. She was billed as Shoshanna the Humming Bird, and Hook sat slumped in his seat, toying with his liquor, watching and

3

figuring ways of making a few rolls of ready money-metal.

Being a loner in the galaxy with allegiances to no one—except, perhaps, to Shaeel the Hermaphrodite—sometimes became tiresome to Hook. He'd scorn any link with any multi-system conglomerate; this more often than not made life excruciating.

As he had surmised, Hook had to step in to take Shoshanna the Humming Bird out of the Palace of FU Delights before the aroused men there could get to her. She appeared completely bewildered. This intrigued Hook. Shashmeeri dancing girls were notorious for their sensuousness.

The place erupted into a cacaphony of shouts and yells, with men of a dozen different races leaping the seats, tearing off their clothes, fighting to be the first. Shoshanna cowered back, her hands to those enormous breasts, each with a pathetic little tinsel-glitter star, her wide eyes wider still with a sudden sick horror of what she had aroused. Hook put his fist into the face of a mal, cracked the head of a Krifman, kicked the feet from under a jernja—those artful aliens had five legs apiece, besides a tail—scooped up Shoshanna and bore her away. She tried to claw his eyes out. He slapped her on that beautifully upholstered rump, and growled: "Still!"

Something about this brown-haired, brown-eyed terrestrial must have aroused absolute terror in her breast, for she fainted. Hook did not smile but he thumped a few more heads, trod over a half-dozen falling bodies, and so fled into the Sonleary night.

By the time he had convinced Shoshanna that her virtue was safe with him, and she'd recovered in her lodgings, Hook was looking for excuses to depart. Shoshanna was trying to earn her living as any Shashmeeri dancing girl could—by dancing.

"Pick a better spot next time, Humming Bird."

"Believe me, Hook—I will!"

4

Her husband had sold up everything they possessed, including Shoshanna's clothes, so that she went to and from work with a tattered old plastivelvet cloak wrapped about her near-nakedness.

"He knew you didn't need clothes in your line of work."

"But he'll come back! He bought a map from a Krifman. Stafiri—that's my husband—has gone to bring back a huge supply of the Virility Gene! We'll be rich! Enormously rich!"

"I hope so," said Ryder Hook. "Where did he go?"

But Shoshanna the Humming Bird had no idea where her husband, Stafiri, had gone to get these supplies of the Virility Gene.

"But he'll come back, Hook. I know he will!"

"Just believe it, girl, just believe it."

She cooked some supper, a tasty light meal that took shape in the ultrasonic cooker from the plastic-wrapped cubes she extracted from the larder, and they ate companionably. The wine, a rosé, did not offend Hook overmuch. The production kit in the lodging house's commonroom dispensed a limited choice; but Shoshanna grew vivacious and excited, and it was very clear that Hook's powerful physique, and clear brown eyes, made her dream wistfully of her vanished husband, Stafiri.

Hook saw that if he wanted to, he could. But, as he had said, he preferred girls to look like human girls from old Earth. He disengaged her white arms and removed his ear from the advances of her lips. They were soft and wanton and her tongue was a marvel. Now, if she'd been a real girl . . .

She'd said good night with a very real puzzlement, pouting, more than a little hurt, and with her two little silver glitter stars in her hands, pathetic.

Ryder Hook heard rumors of the so-called Virility Gene for the third time aboard Stellroute's starship *Vandeneuf* en route to Jundersborg in the Carnaireann Cluster. This time he was traveling in some style, with Shaeel and Karg. As usual, he was one jump ahead of the law, and a bare half a jump ahead of the Boosted Men. If he made it to Jundersborg in one piece he fancied he might stay in one piece long enough to catch his breath.

Sitting in the lounge he listened to the idle conversation.

The name Virility Gene was, of course, something of a misnomer, much used by those sections of the media catering for the less-skilled echelons of the stellar econorgs; but from what Hook gathered on this occasion from the furry little alien from Cailiang, the name fitted in a loose and bowdlerized way.

The habit of continually looking over his shoulder could not easily be broken—he would not wish to break it for he wished to stay alive—even here, in the snug lounge of starship *Vandeneuf*, and Hook felt nothing of the ease he should be feeling in good company, with drinks and music and idleness before him for seven days terrestrial. Stellroutes was a relatively small multi-system conglomerate and a trifle on the shady side, and that suited Hook perfectly.

"It's somewhere there, Taynor Klark," the little Cailiang said to Hook. "A proton speculator told me, and they're not fools."

Hook took his eyes away from the angled mirror that showed him the door to the left. "I agree. They're not. But one hears so much about Virility Genes—how do you disentangle the truth from the imagination?"

A mal seated opposite showed by his facial movements, the way he twirled his tubular ear, that he was seized by a fit of avarice in thus talking of undreamed-of-wealth.

"And this proton speculator was putting credit into it?"

The Cailiang preened his fur, dyed pink and indigo, smoothing it out so that the patterns glowed. "He was."

"As to that," boomed a Krifman, heavily built, authori-

6

tative, wedged into a massively pneumo-upholstered chair. "It really doesn't matter. You can always float a speculation where virility is concerned."

The Cailiang laughed, and the mal nodded, working at his ear. The Krifman settled himself, conscious of the impact he had made. "And," the Krifman continued, nodding with the knowledge of the galaxy. Any econorg would go along with you. They know a good thing when they see one."

For Hook these people represented the assured of the galaxy, people not all of Homo sapiens stock who possessed credit cards and fat bank accounts with the econorgs of their choice. People who would not think twice about stepping on him. He sat back a little, listening, not pushing into the conversation. But the talk drifted to econorgs and their ways, the Virility Gene for the moment absent from the spoken conversation but present in all their minds.

Hook saw with some amusement that the subject had disappeared from the conversation for the intriguing and highly human reason that each one sitting here wanted later to talk privately to the Cailiang. They were like kritchuks sniffing around a hunk of meat, each one waiting until the other made a move so they could snap in from the flanks, destroy the rival and gain the prize for themselves.

He ordered another drink—a plain orange beer—and kept his eyes on the mirror and the door.

The passages out for Shaeel, Karg and Hook had been paid for by Tayniss Thentel. She wasn't as bad as she was painted, and she piled on the face paint too, or so had said Shaeel, the Hermaphrodite, in ves cutting way. Hook had barely escaped from Sykoris with the Boosted Men vengefully sending their agents after him. All Ryder Hook wanted to do in the galaxy was keep his own skin intact, to survive, to make some kind of life for himself, to live.

The Novamen had other ideas.

Hook was forever barred from becoming a Novaman,

and that fact, more than any other, could enrage him. Usually he steered as far away from the Boosted Men as he could.

Shaeel walked into the lounge. Hook saw ves in the mirror.

Shaeel's not-man's not-woman's face showed the compressed lines of tenseness that—quite apart from being unusual for Shaeel—distressed Hook. Hook didn't give a damn for anyone in the entire galaxy, except, perhaps, for Shaeel when the maph wasn't being ves usual sarcastic self.

Of only one thing could Ryder Hook be sure as he rose and walked with vague steps, as though considering another drink or a turn around the promenade deck, and that was that there was no Boosted Man aboard starship *Vandeneuf*.

He would not make a mistake like that. Or—he had not done so up till now.

When they were walking up the deck together, out through the plastiglass doorway and on to the promenade deck, nearly deserted at this time of ship-night, Shaeel said:

"My dear 'ook! Sitting and Drinking, are you? And here is Karg Maintaining an Observation on a character of the most dubious—"

"Someone followed us from Sykoris. That was to be expected."

"You are foolishly credulous, My Great Hairy Masculine Asinine. In my view the painted Ts Thentel contrived our escape Unscathed. Unscathed." The Hermaphrodite habitually spoke in capital letters. "In my view, my dear old Bertie Basthti, we are, all three of us, being Set Up."

"For what?"

The graceful movement of Shaeel's shoulders in the blue coverall could only have been contrived by a being who was neither man nor woman. "That, my dear 'ook, remains one of the Great Unsolved Problems."

"Hasn't Karg sorted him out yet?"

"The good Karg appeared Alarmingly Gentle when I last saw him."

When Karg, who was a F'lovett, looked ferocious, it meant he was normally happy. When he became upset or angry he became docile and inanely cheerful looking.

A light-hearted couple of terrestrials walked past, obviously deeply in love, paying no attention to Hook and the Hermaphrodite. Hook saw them and discarded them from his evil computations. Simple love of that kind seemed to be denied him, he felt, to be reserved for anyone other than himself.

"Let's go and sort out the chancroid, Shaeel."

"With the utmost pleasure."

Hook looked with some favor upon Shaeel. Ves arms and shoulders were smooth and strong, ves waist nipped in and ves hips flared with an insolent feminine swing. The breasts which occasioned so much liveliness in their relationship were decently covered by the blue coverall; but the fab-metal could not conceal the intoxicating sensuousness of their outlines. Yes, Hook decided, not for the first time, it had been a great day for the Galaxy when the genetic scientists of old Earth had created this wonderful race of Hermaphrodites.

There were still ignorant louts who called Hermaphrodites "it" when their correct pronoun was "ves."

Snugged away under Hook's left sleeve the little dis-gel gun could be brought into action by muscular contractions that by neurological surgery gave him instantaneous reactions. Shaeel at this time had a Delling in the same position. The guns were so common as to excite no comment. Their big energy weapons had been locked away for safety in the ship's armory. Only an idiot would care to shoot off a power gun inboard of a spaceship. Hook had met idiots like that before; he wondered, not without a feeling of anger at the waste of time, if the alien on whom Karg was keeping an observation would turn out to be another.

They turned into G-three corridor, empty and clean under the ceiling lighting.

"There's Karg."

One moment the corridor had been empty, the next the squat bulk of the F'lovett appeared, signaling to them. Instantly, Karg vanished again into his cleaning-robot's closet.

A door opened and a Krifman stepped out.

The Krifmans were a race which considered itself to be the best in the galaxy: rough, tough, arrogant, supremely confident. Usually, Hook got on with them quite well. He'd had to thump one or two along the line. He and Shaeel walked along smoothly, talking inconsequentially in an off-hand manner.

The Krifman wore a metal-fab suit that had been smothered in glitter-points, so that he dazzled as he walked. His short red cloak hung from one shoulder to his waist, in the latest fashion. On his belt he carried a holstered Zag, a solid-projectile weapon firing a large bullet at relatively low-velocity, admirable for work inboard of a spaceship. He'd have a credit card surgically implanted in his left wrist, and, without any real doubt, a dis-gel gun on his right. The Krifman barged down the corridor as though he owned Stellroutes starship *Vandeneuf*.

"This must be the feller, my dear 'ook—Abel."

Abel Klark as an alias had been used by Hook before, would be used again. He had many aliases among the stars.

"Sure. Let him go."

"But—!"

"Let's hear what Charlie has to say." Charlie was Karg.

The Krifman marched on, quite clearly with the knowledge implanted in his brain that anyone in his path would step aside. He was so evidently accustomed to deference he could not conceive of receiving anything else.

10

He was, Hook surmised, a high executive of a powerful econorg, no badge or insignia was visible. A dangerous man to make an enemy.

Hook stepped aside.

Shaeel, after a moment of total disbelief, stepped aside also.

They watched the red cloak—more of a cape with its artfully angled slinging—above the glitter suit vanish around the far corner, going on to G-four corridor.

Karg popped out of his closet.

He smiled as though thoroughly amused.

"I'd have finished him off, Hook—"

"Point is, Karg, old friend—what has he done to us to deserve such a fate?"

Karg's thickly chunky body, which came up to Hook's waist, overlapped on both sides of his belt. His arms could crush a beer barrel, as Hook often thought, envisaging that interesting phenomenon with interest, in his mind's eye.

"He's been watching us. Ever since he came aboard."

Karg had come aboard alone. It had seemed to Hook that a Hermaphrodite and a F'lovett traveling together would excite enough memory to give possible trackers a clue. A human being, nondescript in the way Hook cultivated, would arouse no such interest. Even so, Shaeel was called Balson on the passenger list.

"His name is Carshder. He's production executive with SAJ—"

"That miserable bunch!" said Shaeel with proper contempt.

"SAJ is an econorg with considerable power in this section of the galaxy," said Hook, with a mildness that made the others instantly suspicious.

"Yes," Karg went on in his quiet way. "He spacing in to Jundersborg. He's been watching you two—I don't think he's on to me yet—but, if you want my opinion—"

11

"I think," said Shaeel in ves judicial tone that set a man's teeth on edge, "I really think, My Handsome Barrel, such an Eventuality is Most Welcome."

Karg favored the Hermaphrodite with a scowling glare of fury—which meant he was sharing the joke with him—and finished: "All right. So I reckon he's nothing to do with the fun and games back on Sykoris."

Hook had some respect for Karg's proven ability as an investigator. Despite his own harsh self-reliance, he experienced a moment of relief that the Boosted Men had not sent one of their own agents—one of their mindlessly motivated mechanics, one of the Doorn—after him. He needed to get away from all contact with the Boosted Men.

Then Karg brought all that wishful thinking down around Hook's ears in a jagged heap.

"The agent from Sykoris is up on corridor C-five."

Shaeel said: "You are sure, my friend?"

"Sure."

Hook said: "One thing at a time. I don't like the idea of anyone from Sykoris breathing down our necks."

Shaeel giggled at this, and Hook knew the maph was thinking that Karg had precious little neck to be breathed down.

"So we go up there and sort the gonil out, check?"

"Oh, Indisputably, my dear fellow. As we agreed."

"He's a Homo sapiens, like you, Hook." Karg's cheerfulness was now acute. "He's got three enforcers with him. Riffians."

"That should make Life most Interesting," said Shaeel.

"He's planning to hit us just before we make planetfall," said Hook. "Then he and his goons can leave the ship safely. If he hit us too soon everyone would be held for inquiries. He wouldn't like that." Hook stared, at Shaeel and at Karg. "Nor would we."

Karg looked decidedly happy, which meant he was seething with frustration.

"Oh, my dear 'ook! But—wait a minute, My Hairy Masculine Asinine. If we leave them alone we'll never know when they'll hit us."

"Hit them now," said Karg in a cheerful voice.

"There's a way." A thought had struck Hook. "We can hit the gonils and we can blame it on the Krifman."

"How Extraordinarily Apt!"

2

They walked into corridor C-five like two dreams and a nightmare. The nightmare, decided Ryder Hook with some acerbic conviction, could only be himself.

And, Ryder Hook would carry out his threat, too. He'd sort out the men from Sykoris and he'd blame the mess on Carshder, the Krifman. The Krifman pulled enough weight to get out of trouble of that kind and, anyway, he'd most probably be able to prove he hadn't been anywhere near at the time. But in the confusion the trio of dreams and nightmares would be able to slip away.

The corridor showed even more palatial sumptuousness than those on the lower decks. Whoever had sent the man and his three Riffian enforcers had not spared credits. Karg said the Homo sap's name was Michael Michael, and he added in a most meek tone of voice that the fellow looked interestingly dangerous.

Shaeel flicked ves Delling into ves hand a couple of times at this, checking that the neurological implants were satisfactory.

Hook observed, with a feeling that one day, perhaps, he ought to make Shaeel buy one of the more common permanent gun-grafts, where the gun was grafted into the wrist, a tiny growth, so that a mere contraction, a suggestion of a muscular twinge, would shoot the gun instanter. Hook had been down on his luck so often that he preferred to be able to pawn any and everything he possessed should the necessity arise.

The Hermaphrodite saw Hook watching ves and with the luminous empathy of ves race, ve smiled, and said: "I know, my dear feller. And one day, perhaps, you'll go in for a temple-mounted weapon, eyeball-aimed, guaranteed infallible."

"I doubt it. Anyway, they're not so infallible that a marksman can't shoot 'em out, if he's fast enough."

"Cabin Twelve-eleven," said Karg. He sounded as though he might be leading a priestly choir in a great cathedral, and so Hook realized he must address himself to the business in hand.

"We can't just barge in, 'ook!"

"I agree."

"Entice the gonil out," said Karg mellifluously.

"He has, my rotund friend, three enforcers with him. Do you wish me to Send In My Card?"

Karg laughed. "Parenthood's addled your brains, Shaeel."

Hook didn't want these two to start wrangling again over Shaeel's Hermaphroditic offspring. Ve had left ves baby with Thalleyr, the Hermaphroditic father, and Shaeel had said that Thalleyr's baby, whose father was Shaeel, got on famously with ves twin. They were both toddling by now . . .

Mind you, Thalleyr was a member of an econorg, even if it was HMPA, and Hook often wondered, although being too cautious to phrase it in words, just how an organization maph got along with a loner like Shaeel. Hook found it more than remarkable, he found it downright embarrassing, that Shaeel seemed to prefer the company of loners like Karg and Hook to the company of ves own people.

Karg stopped baiting Shaeel and produced from the plastic wallet, color-coded orange, at his belt a penetrug. The tiny cylinder gleamed golden in the suffused illumination. Karg held it in his fingers—fingers astonishingly sensitive for such a massive body—and looked at Hook.

Hook nodded.

"But stand clear instanter, Karg. They're probably screened in there."

"Bound to be, dear fellow. Is It Wise?"

Hook didn't answer. Karg positioned the penetrug and then dinked it against the door. Instantly, he stepped back and to the side.

From the penetrug voices sounded.

One voice carried all the overtones of ruthless authority that inevitably put Hook's nerves on edge; a raw, powerful, hectoring voice.

"And we'll do it when I say, you clunky! Didn't they warn you? This chancroid Hook is murder."

And another voice, the softer hiss of a Riffian.

"So I've heard, Michael Michael. You are in charge of the operation; but the Doorn, Win Fareng, employs us—"

"And you are here to assist me, gonil!"

And a third Riffian voice, sharp now, excited, pointing to immediate action.

"The tell-tale! There's a bug on the door!"

The next second the door smashed open and men raged into the corridor. The three Riffians, bristle-haired aliens who bore a passing resemblance to Homo saps, rushed first. They wore plate-fab clothes, their helmets were locked in place, they were gloved and booted. No dis-gel would deliquesce them. The metal-fab clothing, also, would ward off any bullet-type projectile unless it was a super-high velocity magnum round, and would shed needles like a steel pin cushion.

Shaeel had time to squawk: "What did I say?"

Karg bent even lower and barged into the second Riffian. He reached out and pinned the man's arms, preventing him from using his weapon. The first Riffian already sprawled across the corridor and slammed into the far wall, his neck broken by Hook's blow. Shaeel stopped yelling and kicked the third low down and Hook came back and twisted his neck.

The trio did not rush into the cabin.

Karg's Riffian lay with crushed ribs; but he might live.

Hook picked the Riffian up, ignoring the man's moan, and stood him on his feet. With a rippling explosion of muscles and sinews, Hook propelled the Riffian through the door.

The man's body was shredded by a salvo of rounds from a magnum.

Before the body fell Hook followed it in. He saw the cabin in a single all-encompassing glance. Michael Michael stood by the table, the magnum in his hand now wavering down as he recognized just who it was he had shot to pieces. Hook although moving in what was slow time to a Boosted Man, gave Michael Michael no chance. He dived low. He hit the man around the waist. Such was the force with which Hook forced down on the gun wrist he shattered it. Bones gleamed pinkly. Michael Michael screamed and Hook got his legs under him, jacknifed up, chopping Michael Michael in the throat.

Shaeel and Karg dragged the other two bodies in and piled them on one side.

Karg said with a stupendously angry tone: "They didn't even wait to see what it was all about—the bastards would have shot us down without another thought."

"So they would," said Ryder Hook. "So they would."

Shaeel was looking around the cabin. Ve wrinkled up ves nose and brushed ves auburn hair back from ves face.

"These Swan-Durk magnums are supposed to be

silenced; but I think enough noise has been made, my dear 'ook, to raise the alarm."

"Yes," said Hook. "All out."

Outside Karg was looking cheerful again. "What about that other Krifman fool, Carshder, we were going to frame for this?"

Hook was busy locking the cabin door.

"We'll tie that in inside an hour."

"An hour," Shaeel gave ves opinion free. "Michael Michael will have woken by then."

"That's what I'm counting on."

They started off for the lounge. Hook could feel no sympathy for Michael Michael and his henchmen. For one thing they were employed by the Doorn. But, most importantly, they were going to kill Hook, Shaeel and Karg. If anyone tried to kill Hook he would stop them, if he could, and if in the process they wound up dead, that was just bad luck for them. Hook did not fancy being killed, least of all by curds like these. He felt no one should be allowed to kill him; he was somewhat old-fashioned in his views.

The ship's officers of *Vandeneuf*, for instance, would have been powerless. Reporting a potential assassination to them would not have stopped that assassination. Hook had had experience of that before. So he marched quickly to the lounge to implement the rest of this distasteful business.

The lounge was less crowded than it had been when Hook had sat talking about the Virility Gene. People were drifting away to their cabins or state rooms, some cradling a last drink, others with the night's amorous activities all worked out. The Krifman still sat blockily in his chair, and the mal, busily twirling his ear tube, sat with him. The two were playing cards, and Hook wouldn't have given odds on either one to outcheat the other. The little furry Cailiang was missing; then Hook noticed him, and cursed.

He was engaged in a deep conversation at a small side

table with the Krifman, Carshder. Hook had been counting on finding Carshder alone. The Krifman had made no friends on the voyage so far, and he was sailing alone.

"It's your play, my dear feller."

"Hook will think of something, he always does."

Hook glanced at the bulkhead-mounted clock keeping standard ship's time, calibrated out in terrestrial minutes and seconds. They had forty-six minutes to go. Hook knew to a nicety the values of his blows.

A crowd of giggling people, a hodge-podge of a dozen different planetary types, a weird mixture of fur and feather, skin and scale, hopped and walked and wriggled from the lounge. They were laughing and talking, still buoyed by the pleasant evening. Hook became aware of an alien standing to one side and smiling upon that brilliant scene.

Yet to Hook's acute senses the fact was instantly obvious that although this alien, a welpac, appeared to be giving his whole attention to the fun and games, his real concern lay with the Cailiang and Carshder.

Now that was interesting.

Through that old Powerman Project of RCI from which Hook had been so ignominiously ejected, and which had given him some of the phenomenal properties of his body, he was able to hear extraordinarily well at considerable distances. Now, even though the departing passengers were kicking up a hell of a racket close by, Hook was able to overhear a large part of the few words Carshder and the Cailiang exchanged.

"...no good your pestering me, Taynor Carshder. You have all the information I know."

"And I'm paying you well for it. Have you told anyone else?"

The Cailiang hesitated. To even the most naive greenhorn in the galaxy the hesitation was most eloquent.

Then he said: "Of course not, Taynor Carshder. The

agreement was to supply you with the information. I've done that. There's nothing else."

"It's easy to say that."

The two went wrangling on.

Hook's thoughts revolved bleakly around the central thesis: "Hurry it up, you nurdling curds!" He could wait no longer.

He nudged Shaeel.

"The lounge is empty enough. I'll take Carshder. You and Karg take out the Cailiang."

"The Pleasure is mutual—but Undeniable."

Hook took a step forward—and changed the direction of his movement away from the two at the side table and toward the dispensor. Shaeel bumped into him, and said something highly disparaging. Karg remained where he was.

Hook experienced the sense of everything going wrong again, he seemed to be wading through molasses. Nothing he touched on this trip seemed to be going right.

The two had risen, Carshder tall and bulky above the furred Cailiang. They moved to the door. And as they did so, the welpac moved. He moved with the fluid rapidity of his race. Well-built and lithe, the welpacs, with two arms and two legs and a flat stump of a tail. Their faces showed two eyes set slanting beneath bunched eyebrows, their noses insignificant, their mouths narrow and downcurved in their wedge-shaped jaws. They affected their hair in extravagant styles, coiled and plaited and threaded with gems and precious metals. More often than not the precious metals were mere simulacra.

Now the welpac moved, his tail hard and jutting to the rear, flung himself on Carshder.

Shaeel said something about fellers needin' a lesson in common decency. Karg barreled in from the side.

Ryder Hook wanted to stand with his hands on his hips, his legs braced wide apart, throw his head back and bellow his laughter. His two comrades descended on the welpac, tripped him, twisted his arms up his back and so held him, helpless, for Carshder's inspection.

The big Krifman took it all in his stride.

"This feller was about to Deprive you of your Faculties," said Shaeel.

Karg said nothing but took another turn on the welpac's sinewy arms.

"You—" Carshder had himself under immediate control. "I see. You have my thanks, taynors. I do not know him; but I am sure the captain will find space in his brig for a would-be assassin."

"As serious as that, taynor?" said Shaeel, all eyes and mouth. "It seems your Person is Indeed Valuable."

Carshder gave the Hermaphrodite a quick and hard glance; and Hook groaned again at the eloquence of Shaeel. One day, for sure, ve'd put ves big foot in ves big mouth.

"We'll take him to the cap'n," said Karg in a ferocious voice.

Hook stepped forward.

"I am glad to see you are safe, Taynor Carshder." He looked around. The little furry Cailiang had vanished. Hook made his harsh features stretch into a gargoyle smile. "Perhaps it would be advisable for us to escort you to your cabin."

"That will not be necessary. You have my thanks. I will credit your account with a suitable reward money—"

Carshder stopped speaking. He stopped speaking abruptly. Hook had reached out gently, oh, so gently, and knuckled him behind the ear. The big Krifman collapsed into Hook's arms.

"And about time, too, Abel!" said Shaeel. Ve spoke loudly. "The Krifman's attempts to hold liquor have Proved Fruitless."

Hook saw the girl looking at them, not sure what was

21

going on. She was Homo sap, and rather sweet, in a lime-green dress and silver-glitter. Hook's inhumanly atrocious attempts at a smile must have frightened her, for she let out a little squeak, her hands to her mouth.

"Please do not be alarmed, tayniss," called Shaeel. "This Krifman suffers from what the technically minded among us observers of the human condition call Blotto."

The girl took her hands away. She laughed.

The welpac, struggling unavailingly in the grip of Karg, was mouthing away.

"Let go, you great fat barrel of batter! I wasn't trying to kill the gonil! Let go!"

"Stay still, fren," said Karg.

"Oh, I'll admit I wanted to bust him on the nose! But it's not an assassination! Dolt! Imbecile!"

Karg just screwed up a little tighter.

The girl looked puzzled again.

Hook said: "Nevertheless, Taynor Carshder. I will escort you to your cabin." He started to walk off with the unconscious body of the Krifman supported by one muscular arm, as though Carshder was dead drunk.

"Is he all right?" called the girl.

"Perfectly, thank you, tayniss. A little shut eye and he'll be as right as rain."

"Not like," said the girl, essaying a small joke, "the rain on Sculin."

"It's unlikely."

Hook dragged Carshder away.

The welpac still, amazingly enough, managed to struggle in Karg's grip, and somehow, Karg's grip slipped. Somehow, Hook fancied, Karg just hadn't given the welpac the real attention he deserved. The welpac half-slipped free. He tried to loop one of his fists into Karg's pugnacious eye. Karg's face would have frozen a nuclear pile, which meant he was enjoying himself. He took another grip with one hand, blocked the blow with the other, said: "Gamey little tangle-pants, ain't you?"

The welpac gave a last violent wrench, experienced the sensation of trying to shift a six-meter mulybdenum core out of gran-cement, and gave up. "You haven't won, fren," the welpac said. "This is only round one."

"Great Salvor!" said Karg, with such an inimical leer he must have been one huge chuckle. "Preserve me from that."

Reaching corridor C-five Hook listened on the penetrug still inconspicuously fastened on its magnetic ring to the door. All quiet on the Doorn front. He shoved the door open and went in; but he went in with Cashder draped over his chest—just in case—and his dis-gel gun out and in his hand. Michael Michael and his remaining enforcer slumbered. Hook dumped Carshder down and stepped back surveying the scene.

Yes. Most decidedly. A delicate touch of the Hook flair for artistic decoration was called for here.

Hook went to work, dragging unconscious bodies, arranging them, placing them so that they told a story.

Anyone coming into the cabin would see instantly that Carshder and Michael Michael had been engaged in an argument, the enforcers had intervened, there had been a nasty little fracas—with these unhappy results.

For Ryder Hook to do these things meant only that he sought his own survival—his own and that of Shaeel and Karg—and if a gruesome jollity turned off those stay-at-homes of the galaxy, all Hook could do was to sympathize with them, acknowledge his own faults, and then get on with the necessities of life.

The last few touches completed—the removal of the goons' helmets gave a more convincing tableau—Hook stepped back. He did not admire his handiwork. But he had to own that it was most artistic, most.

Shaeel and Karg would have understood at once and with

the intuitive comprehension of the galactic adventurer. Not for the first time Hook regretted Karg had not managed to snitch three transceivers. He would have to go and find out what those two were up to instead of calling them up.

He stepped out into the corridor, twitched the penetrug off the door, heard a soft and furtive footfall at his back and so dived full length, rolled and sprang up, his dis-gel gun in his hand.

The jolly girl with the sweet face stood staring at him in open-mouthed wonder. Her lime-green dress had been caught back against her thighs by the arresting of her walk, and she really did look nice. Hook didn't care what he looked like.

He could have said: "People get dead quick doing that."

Instead he let the electronic circuits slide the gun back up under his sleeve.

The girl said: "They're all in it together, Rhus."

From the doorway to the cabin where the girl paused stepped the blocky Krifman who talked so authoritatively among the others, with the mal and the Cailiang who had mentioned the Virility Gene. His face showed controlled power now, directed to anger and decision.

"You're right, Sharon."

In the infinitesimal instant that Hook knew he had blundered, that he should not have let the gun slip back, the Krifman fired. A blossoming cloud of nothingness overtook Ryder Hook in the stun-gun's blast. The thing was set to full power and Ryder Hook's consciousness, despite that skull of his, vanished like a dissolving dream at dawn.

3

The metal whimpered.

The sound told Ryder Hook that the life-shell was on its last legs. He felt the relaxing after effects of the stun-gun blast leaking away from his brain, leaving a dull and annoying ache that would persist for an hour or two without medication.

He levered himself up against the bulkhead, and the vibrating metal whimpered down the scale.

He understood what had happened and, if he cared to think carefully about it, the whys and wherefores, also.

"You feeling better now, Taynor Klark?"

Hook eyed the welpac with some animosity.

"What the hell are you in here for, fren?"

"The same reason as you, I suggest." The welpac did not look uncomfortable. He wedged his wide shoulders into the angle of hull and bulkhead and took out a packet of stim gum. He stripped the plastic away and offered some to Hook. Hook waved it away.

"So what's the reason, fren?"

"My name is Brett—or, at least, that is what you may call me for now. As to the reason, since we are here and therefore would seem to have failed, I shall tell you. The Cailiang, Fenton, claimed to know the secret of the whereabouts of the planet producing the Virility Gene—"

"Save it," said Hook. "I'm not in the market for buying treasure maps."

"You should have been—" began Brett, then he paused His elaborate hair-styling had been badly mussed, and he took out a pneumo-comb and brush and went to work on its piled curls. Then: "You're not trying to tell me you weren't after the map?"

"Not since I was six and bought an iridium-mine map."

"I see."

The welpac went on fussing with his hair and studying Hook. Hook, for his part, stood up and looked about. The cabin of the life shell was more spartan than most; but it held all the essentials to keep people alive in space—for a measured amount of time. It was perfectly clear to Hook after a couple of minutes reading of the instruments that the whimpering metal had told a true story. The life-shell was dying.

"We're alone in the shell, Taynor Klark. So—"

Hook turned his face on Brett and Brett shut up.

So what had happened to Shaeel and Karg? Were they even alive? Shaeel could look after ves skin, and Karg was a dynamo both of destruction and self-preservation. Hook wouldn't believe them dead until he saw them dead.

"That bitch Sharon," Brett said, speaking without looking at Hook. "She and that gonil of a Krifman Rhus. They came out on top—or so they think." And then, surprising Hook, Brett the welpac giggled. He clearly knew something that he regarded as a good joke, something that amused him enormously.

Ryder Hook was in no mood to share the joke.

The life-shell's radio communications had been casually smashed. Someone had taken the nearest hard object to the panels and stoved them in. A metalloy spanner, used to chock the manual air-lock seals, lay on the decking. Hook didn't even bother to pick it up.

"Oh, yes, fren," said the welpac, still laughing. "We're done for. I know that Sharon lady-bitch. She doesn't like to soil her hands with killing. Even when her bodyguard Rhus could do it for her, if she's around she doesn't like it."

"I know something else she won't like when we meet up," said Hook, considering the wreckage of the radios.

As an electronics expert—among many other expertises necessary to survival in this whirling galaxy of the hundred and first century—Hook felt the challenge of the ruined circuits. The drive continued to function in a half-hearted way. The life-support system also continued, although the air tasted metallic and flat, strictly down-level substandard Hook knew the board, all right, a simple layout suitable for broadcasting on emergency bands if the life-shell had to eject from its parent starship. Sharon and her henchman, Rhus, had activated it from far from humanitarian reasons.

There were components scattered about, some from here, some from there, sufficiently undamaged for Hook to see a way of lashing up a board that might punch out a distress signal for perhaps half a parsec or so on the ultra-channels used by interstellar shipping. He went to work.

Brett stopped laughing and said: "You're wasting your time, Klark."

Hook ignored him.

If people wanted to fight and cheat and kill for the secret of the Virility Gene—that was all IQ, provided they did not involve Ryder Hook in their intrigues. Since he'd quite clearly been flung into the middle of a conspiracy he felt obligated to find out just who had been doing the flinging and show them what a set of weapons placed in the most suitable target might do for their health.

Sharon and Rhus.

And Carshder was in on it, too.

Sharon had thought that Hook was scheming with Carshder, seeing the affectionate way Hook had carried off the dead-drunk Krifman, and she no doubt was perfectly convinced of an explanation she had thought up to please herself as to why Hook had taken Carshder to Michael Michael's cabin, and what they had been up to there. Hook felt it singularly appropriate that Sharon might have second thoughts when the tableau in Michael Michael's cabin was eventually revealed.

These damn people of the galaxy, filled with the might and power of their econorgs, all scheming and struggling away for power and more power, for luxury and more luxury. All Ryder Hook wanted to do was stay alive—oh, yes, and have a little fun and games as well, whenever they could be managed.

"How are you doing, Klark?"

Hook, deep into the intricacies of higher space-time continuum quanta, fiddling with the circuits that would throw a pulsed signal across space, and, at the same time, grunching away about idiots who sought always for more power and wealth in the galaxy, did not reply to the welpac. The marriage of theory and practice had always fascinated him. My God! They'd done some shotgun work on his body, when they'd rigged him for a heavy gravity planet on the Powerman Project. Many of his proteins had been reinforced, replaced, adapted, with metallic elements. And there had been more jiggery-pokery when Earth's Armed Services had implanted those organic circuits in his skull. Well, if he couldn't get this mess sorted he'd have to go on net to some local apparat and risk having his brains fried in his skullbones.

Brett couldn't stop picking the sore.

"You're wasting your time, fren. We're done for. No air, no food, no drink. The drive's collapsing. We're gonna drift

28

in space, for ever, a spatial Flying Dutchman, for ever and ever—"

"Shut your face, fren," Hook didn't bother to specify what would happen if the welpac didn't. His tone of voice, alone, eloquently conveyed that information.

Ten minutes, terrestrial, later, Hook stepped back. The normal one eighth of a gravity artifical gravity remained, sure indication that the power pile was still functioning. There would be energy for the radio call. He'd be using only a little and yet what he used would materially decrease the reserves. They skimped on these life-shells, did starship builders. Mind you, they could put up a case for that. So few starships ever had accidents that some starship builders, members of powerful econorgs, were always yapping on about rescinding the strict space laws

"You haven't—?"

The answer Hook gave to that was to settle in the operator's seat, feed in the power—carefully—balance the jury-rigged set out. When it was working to his satisfaction he sent out a standard emergency signal. He blipped it out half a dozen times.

The enforcers who had smashed up the radio had left the tape facility undamaged—what was the use of that without a radio to hook it into?—although they had thoroughly smashed the astrogational instruments and panels. Hook didn't know where in space he was, although common sense told him they had not traveled far from Stellroutes starship *Vandeneuf*. He set up a homing signal, taped up the distress call, fed them both into a loop and left the set broadcasting.

Brett slumped back.

"I wouldn't have believed that if I hadn't seen it with my own eyes. You an electronics man?"

"No," said Ryder Hook. "I'm a zoo keeper."

"Yes, very funny. I like a guy who likes a joke."

Brett was already feeling better, Hook saw, perfectly

confident now that the distress call would be picked up in short order and they'd be the heroes of a dramatic space rescue. Hook would believe that when it happened.

The storage compartments revealed the tag end of the rationscale of supplies. Someone had been filching from the life-shell, secure in the knowledge inhabiting their tiny minds that the shell would never, ever be used.

Ryder Hook had no time for inefficiency—a perfectly normal outlook in a society that spread throughout space and was dependent on perfectly functioning equipment to ensure its survival—and also he did not like petty thievery if it served no good end.

"Bunch of regurgitated womb fugitives!" He slammed the pack of compressed rations down and fed a chunk into the processor. He was hungry. "If I was a captain of a starship and found any member of my crew pilfering emergency rations—"

"You'd what, Klark? Burn 'em down?"

Hook turned to glare at the welpac.

"Burn 'em down? No. That'd be too quick for the bastards."

Brett's eyes blinked in that feline way of welpacs.

"By Pakveil! I believe you mean it!"

There was no answer to that Hook cared to make.

He went back to the lavatory and locked the door. The idea that Brett might kill him in order to make the supplies of air and food last had to be considered. He checked the dis-gel gun. Sharon hadn't overlooked that. The magazine was empty.

Well, if the fates cavorting around the old galaxy were to be trusted—and they weren't, they weren't—then Sharon would also have emptied Brett's wrist gun. That was something Hook must take notice of. Anything to do with preserving his own skin must be treated with great seriousness.

Back in the cabin Brett was busily engaged in serving the

processed food. It was barely palatable, a kind of basic mix of essentials designed to keep people alive whilst they waited to be rescued. Brett licked his fingers and made a face.

"Why any curd would want to steal this stuff beats me."

"Anything has a price in the galaxy," said Hook, sitting down and reaching for a bowl and spoon. "Some poor devil would be willing to pay for this stuff. Pay in whatever he had available." He did not need to embroider.

They both ate in silence.

When Brett had finished he sat back and considered Hook.

"You strike me as a rough character, Taynor Klark. I've seen a bit of the galaxy. My econorg is Welton's—at the moment—and you may know of them. They're small."

"Yes."

"So sometimes I get pushed around. Either Welton's get bigger in a hurry or I change."

"It's not easy to change, Brett. Multi-system conglomerates are jealous of the prerogatives they hand out for their favorites. They won't take a changer without plenty of credits. And then—"

"Yes! Then his own econorg won't want to see him go. They won't release his credits easily, unless he gets cash for them in advance."

"So?"

"So if you intend to kill me, Taynor Klark, think again. I'm not a soft office worker."

Hook laughed.

"I've no intentions of killing you, Taynor Brett. To be honest—" The irony of that might not be lost in this welpac, either!— "I'm intrigued by all this nonsense about the Virility Gene. If anyone does to me what Sharon and Rhus did, I reckon I'm owed compensation."

"And would a beating-up, perhaps a killing, recompense you?"

"No. I don't go around beating people up. Do you?"

31

Brett was taken aback.

"Certainly not. Unless—"

"Unless what?"

"Unless they've done me dirt—"

"So there's your answer. Vengeance is mine, saith the Lord. I'm no god. I'm just a mortal human being."

"Yes. A Homo sap. Well, I'm a Homo welpac, and proud of it. We know how to keep a feud running."

"I wish you joy of it. I make it an invariable rule to avoid unpleasantness whenever possible."

This welpac had Ryder Hook summed up fairly well, for he said, with something of a triumphant leer: "And you damn well see to it that the whenever possible happens as often as possible. Check?"

"If you say so."

So a kind of unarmed truce was arrived at; for by this time Hook felt reasonably confident that Brett was disarmed, as he was himself.

About midnight ship's time, and by the chronometer the third day, the air became foul enough for them both to know that time was running very short. There was still a sufficiency of rations—Hook had always had a partiality for a sufficiency at parties—so the air would be the factor that would kill them. The lack of oxygen, rather. The recycling units went on pumping and cycling; but the oxygen was not being replaced. Hook checked the reserves and made the simple calculation that they had eleven and three quarter more hours left. Terrestrial hours. Brett harrumphed, and said that was fifteen of the planet he called home, Lemphale. Then he laughed. Hook was not amused.

"So I've got fifteen more hours left in this Pakveil-cursed galaxy, Klark, and you've only got eleven and three quarters. I rather like that."

Hook glared at Brett.

"You're a real comedian, as a friend of mine would say."

However, there was something about this atrocious welpac that was getting to Ryder Hook, some quality of cocky unput-downableness that he did not exactly admire as regard with a wry caution and affection. Hook felt it a real shame their relationship, so recently begun, was to be so quickly ended.

Five hours thirty seven minutes later—or seven and a half hours later according to Brett—the air hung like some foul sewer miasma in the passenger cabin. Hook got up on to his legs and checked the radio was still thumping out the distress call and the homing signal. *Vandeneuf* had been a perfectly ordinary starship, keeping to the recognized stellar routes through the star-clusters in this sector of space. The life-shell had been hurled away and, breaking through into sub-light speeds, could be no real distance from where it had begun. So they were still in the shipping lanes. Therefore a starship should be along any second now.

Shouldn't it?

If she didn't come soon, she needn't bother.

Despite the fact that he had more hours by his own reckoning to go, Brett was suffering badly. His chest heaved jerkily, and sweat ran down past his down-curved mouth, glittering through the unshaven wedge-shaped jaws. His tiny nostrils flared as he gulped stale air. Soon, Hook fancied, the welpac might very well be tearing at his chest and throat, whimpering, moaning, flinging his body in ungainly convulsions. Well, Hook did not like the effects of oxygen starvation, either.

The hours ticked by. More and more often Hook checked that the distress call continued to broadcast out into space. He had no way of knowing if a ship had already picked up the signal, was letting down out of her starflight envelope, was vectoring to make contact with the tiny hull of the life-shell. He would only know when he heard the thump from outside, when they matched locks, when they started

33

pumping in the beautiful, wonderful, heavenly fresh air.

"How much longer?" croaked Brett.

Hook said: "Two hours."

"Terrestrial, I suppose?"

Hook saved his breath.

But the welpac wanted to talk. The effort of opening that mouth of his, of framing words, of thinking, of talking, tired him; but he insisted. Hook thought the welpac was scarcely thinking at all. Neither of them had the energy to eat but they kept drinking copiously. Brett rambled on. Hook only half-listened. This, it seemed to him, was a damned undignified way of saying goodbye to the whirlpool of stars.

". . . lot nonsense, they always said. I always half believed. We're gonna die, Hook, die—"

"Did you say Hook?"

"Hook? No. No, I didn't say Hook. I said Klark. Abel Klark. Course I didn't say Ryder Hook."

Hook crawled across the deck toward Brett. He lifted his hands to the welpac's neck. He was breathing in gasps that sent stabs of scarlet pain into his brain.

"You said Hook, you gonil!"

Brett's mind was wandering. He giggled, weakly.

"I seen you before. In a joint on the hashish worlds. You busted a guy's nose—you can't do that to me, I'm a welpac." Brett giggled again, maundering. "Li'l joke. Calling you Taynor Klark. But I knew. An' I kep' my mouth shut, Hook. Didn' let on . . ."

Hook took his clutching fingers away.

If they were both going to die from oxygen starvation he had no wish to speed the welpac on his way. The clunkhead would only be waiting at the gate of heaven with a crowbar ready to hit him. No, much better make him wait, get to the gate first, ready to deal with him when he arrived . . . Much better . . .

No wonder the curd had been giggling earlier. But—Brett

wasn't a real curd, was he? Not a gonil. No, he was just a clunky of a welpac, ready for a joke and a spot of mayhem and what he could make...

"...That curd Cailiang Fenton sold me the secret. Me! And that lady-bitch, Sha—Shar—Sharon—and her punk Krifman were froze out. An' then that sonofabitch Carshder shipped in, with more money—Fenton was scared clean through. An' I fooled 'em all..."

"So you know where they produce the Virility Gene," said Hook. "Much good that's doing you now."

"I know! I know the place—Shyle, that's what those crafty gonils call it, Shyle—an' I know how to get th' Vilgene—*I know*!"

"If you were destined for a grave, Brett, you'd take that knowledge with you."

"I know!" Brett reared up from the bulkhead, his wedge-shaped jaws splattered with saliva, his up-slanting eyes wild. His hair had fallen and collapsed into a bird's-nest mess. "I know! I can be rich! Richer than anyone can imagine—an' I c'n tell Welton's where to—where to shove it! The Vilgene will give me everything!"

"It can't give you life now—and shut up! Save the oxy, what's left of it."

Brett opened his curved mouth to snarl back at Hook.

A loud and gonging thump sounded from the airlock, reverberating through the hull.

Both men sat in stunned stupefaction.

For a moment Hook could not remember why that clanging concussion of metal against metal was so important.

He managed to stand up. His head thumped and gyrated. Now was the time to call out on the nearest net, get someone here, risk having his brains fried in his skull. But that bump from outside. *Outside!*

He needn't risk calling out with the organo-electronic

circuits implanted in his head by EAS. Someone was out there now, someone summoned by the distress signal. He staggered across to the airlock inner valve. The teleplate above showed the rind of stars occulted by a dark bulk. Another ship had locked on.

The sense of what was happening penetrated through the sluggish veil of oxygen starvation in Brett's mind. He crawled after Hook.

"Open it, Hook! *Open it*!"

On the teleplate appeared a face.

Hook saw the face.

He stared at it and the sickness in his stomach almost made him vomit.

A cheerful face showed on the plate, looking in, concerned, now, over the state of the people in the life shell. A face with green skin and two green eyes, fierce upright fuzz of bristle hair, with wide and mobile lips that, as Hook knew, were normally curved up in a genial smile, that face showed true care for the safety of life.

"Open the valves, Hook!"

The face looked worried. The lips opened. Over the speaker the voice said. "We have locked on and are in your airlock, fren."

Brett heaved himself up. He staggered against Hook. His hands scrabbled in maniacal desperation for the manual airlock controls. He was gasping and retching, and his hands shook so that he had to hang on to the manuals; but he held on, and he began to open the airlock inner valve.

"No," said Ryder Hook.

He pushed Brett away, valved the lock shut.

"The gonil! We'll die! Die! Open the door and let fresh air in! Hurry, you curd, before we're dead"

"No," said Ryder Hook. "I will not open the valve."

4

It seemed to Ryder Hook he must be getting to be an old galactic adventurer, and tired.

Brett tried to kick him in the groin. The welpac's foot moved slowly, like a leaf drifting from the shaking trees of home. Hook blocked the blow. If Brett was experiencing the pain in the head that Hook was suffering in his, no wonder the welpac was frantic

"Open it! Open it!"

"They're chlors, Brett!"

The green voice in the green face said: "We are bringing pumping equipment and oxy cylinders as fast as we can." The green eyes showed concern. "Please do not let the welpac open the inner valve. It would be—unpleasant."

"He won't."

Brett flopped over and glared up at the teleplate.

"Chlors!" he said. Through all the pain that tore at his skull he still managed to look indignant, a common expression among races who fancied their own self-esteem. "Well, you big gnarly sap—why didn't you tell me!"

"You were in somewhat of a hurry."

They were panting for the last molecules of oxygen now,

their faces beginning to change color as the blood vessels reacted. Brett slumped down again, tearing continuously at his coverall neck.

"My head's going to come off any second! Pakveil! Tell the chlors to hurry, Hook!"

The green voice from the green face said: "We are hurrying, fren. We do not wish to introduce our atmosphere into your life shell. And we do not, most certainly do not, want to let any of your air into our ship."

"I understand," said Hook, gasping, feeling his cranium spinning on solid aluminized treads around his skull. "Just hurry it up, fren."

"Our engineer is highly competent."

Brett let out a moan. "Just my luck! Pakveil knows! To be rescued by a ship with incompatible atmosphere!"

The chlor engineer in the other ship would be drilling a hole through the life-shell's outer airlock valve—not as difficult a task as one might expect, judging from the shoddy construction of the shell—and when he had threaded an oxyhose through, they'd close up the valve, evacuate the oxy-nitrogen-trace elements air which was a lethal poison to the two in the shell. Then the air lock would be flooded with oxygen and the inner valve could be opened.

The chlors were a decent enough race of beings, friendly most of the time, awkward customers when riled—and didn't that description fit a goodly proportion of the peoples of the galaxy? It wasn't their fault they had evolved on a planet in which substantial trace elements of a gas with effects similar to arsine existed in the atmosphere. Arsine itself took a little time to thicken and coagulate the blood of people unaccustomed to breathing it in with their oxygen and nitrogen and other rare gases; but the derivation to be found in the chlor's atmosphere were deadly in double quick time. It was tit for tat, too; ordinary terrestrial air would kill a chlor as fast as his air would kill a terrestrial.

Hook and Brett waited, sweating it out, seeing the black specks dancing before their eyes, growing weaker—dreaming strange undersea dreams that trailed away into the encroaching grayness of final dissolution.

The inner airlock valve opened and a gush so pure, so cold, so gorgeous, burst through that both men wallowed.

They guzzled the oxygen like drunks.

Presently they could quiet down and realize they had not died, that this time they had cheated death.

As Brett the welpac said: "It was a near thing, Hook—or should I say Abel Klark?—and something I don't want to have to go through again, believe you me."

"Nor me," said Hook, to whom the experience was hardly novel.

After a time Hook went to the space suit lockers and dragged out the oxy cylinders which had all been expended. He made arrangements with the chlors to have the bottles go across through the lock—the care with which the cycling was done outdid that given to it even when they were valving to go into space—to be filled and returned. The chlor ship was a simple Hard passenger. A small drive and control and cabin unit housed the five-man crew. This unit towed a massive string of balloons, each filled with the frozen cargo of human bodies traveling Hard. They were all either chlors or people of races who could accept the chlor's atmosphere.

Then Hook braced himself for the bad news.

The Star-Hard was aimed for Laband. The journey time at relatively low starflight velocity would take three months Terran. Hook frowned. He asked that a signal be sent to Stellroutes starship *Vandeneuf* inquiring tactfully about Balson and Charley. At this time payment for the use of radio facilities was not mentioned. The reply puzzled Hook.

"Balson and Charley all IQ. Request Abel Klark stay away from contact."

Puzzled, unable to determine if Shaeel and Karg had

really sent the reply, Hook badgered another signal out. This time the reply was merely a repeat of the first.

"They're dead, Hook," said Brett. "Sharon couldn't hold her chopperman Rhus back that time. Or," he added, preening his squabby tail. "It could be Carshder."

"I don't think a chopperman like Rhus could get to Balson."

"You don't have much experience of the galaxy, do you, Hook?" Brett guffawed. He had been saved; he was taking it easy. "A good chopperman can get to anyone." He left his tail and went to work seriously on his hair with his pneumo comb and brush. "I heard a story about Jack Kinch, once. Now there," he added reflectively, "Is a real chopperman!"

Hook didn't bother to ask about Jack Kinch. As far as he knew only a few people in the bureau of Earth's Armed Services knew that the failure, Ryder Hook, had for a time been the galaxy's number one assassin, Jack Kinch. Now he was simply Ryder Hook, out to keep his nose clean and stay alive.

Brett rambled on about the miraculous way Jack Kinch had gone in and out of an impregnable fortress. "As a galactic assassin, he's the tops, Hook."

"Yes? How many galaxies has he assassinated lately?"

Brett wasn't offended. "I'm a university graduate. Ask me how many universities I've graduated in my time, Hook."

"Yes, I know. It's simple semantics. I just wondered."

The chlor captain spoke to them over the teleplate.

"We want to know what you want to do, Taynor Klark. If you wear your suits you can come aboard."

"Is your oxy supply sufficient to let us live here?"

"Probably. Our engineer can easily calculate that. But can you pay for it, Taynor Klark?"

Brett cut in, speaking quickly, breathily.

"I can pay. My credit's good with Welton's."

"Welton's." There came the buzz of conversation, then the captain turned back. "Agreed."

When the green face on the teleplate died, Hook said to the welpac: "When will you want the cash for my half of the oxy?"

"Cash?"

Hook drew up the blue coverall sleeve over his left wrist.

Brett left off combing his hair. He puckered up that down-curving mouth.

"You are a prize clunkhead, Hook."

"So I'm told."

"So you're in my debt to what could be a three-month supply of oxygen?"

"So it seems."

"I've often wondered what it would be like, to be a loner. Changing names and all. But—" he shivered. "But it's not for me. I like the strength of an econorg about me, even if it is only measly old Welton's."

"It takes all sorts to make a galaxy."

The chlor captain came back with the news that they could remain in the life-shell and be supplied with oxygen. The chlors were making contact with a compatible-type starship and if they could find one willing to drop down out of starflight envelope to pick them up were prepared to do the same as well.

"This is very good of you, captain," said Hook.

"I know. We'll have to charge you out to Welton's, though. The company will insist."

And the company as a unit of a multi-system conglomerate would have to do as the econorg said. It was all a geared system, for those with credit card facilities with the econorgs of the galaxy.

"That's right, captain," said Hook. "You do that."

Brett said: "You're really running into my debt, Hook."

"What makes you so sure I'll pay you?"

The lines of Brett's welpac face hardened and changed and his squat tail hit the deck where he sat with a drum-thump.

"I read you, Hook. I read the kind of man you are, sap or not. You pay off a debt."

"You came to the same conclusion earlier, I remember."

"Get off my back, Hook! You owe me."

"Sure."

For now, Brett was willing to let it lie. As a man who had knocked about the galaxy and who knew a trick or two, he wasn't prepared to bring any potential argument to a head in circumstances where he did not have every opportunity possible to win. Hook knew this. Also, Hook knew that there was a streak in the welpac that might make of him either a most dangerous adversary or a most highly esteemed companion. It would be up to Brett which one he chose.

The chlor captain was as good as his word and three days—terrestrial—later, Hook and Brett transferred to H.G.L. Starship *Zacatecas*. The two bid the green-faced captain and his crew farewell with genuine expressions of thanks, after full details had been taken from Brett's wrist credit card.

Zacatecas turned out to be a third-class starship, well-appointed, reasonably fast, comfortable, and with a passenger list that came only half way down the printed form available and which indicated she was running half empty.

"We're half-full, Taynor Brett," said the captain, a pudgy mal, twirling his ear lobes. "We're glad to have you aboard."

Hook wondered what this cheerful captain would have done had he been running the parsecs full. It seemed expedient not to inquire. Further deductions were made against Brett's credit with Welton's.

Brett said, very firmly: "We'll share a cabin. Second class."

"But," said the captain, spreading his hands, smiling. "I have a couple of very nice singles, first class, available—"

"Double. Second."

The captain's smile slipped a little. "As you wish."

In the cabin, a typical example of H.G.L.'s third-class ship, second-class passenger, decor, Brett thumped his tail down on the most convenient bed, and glared at Hook.

"I'm paying for this little lot, Hook! You needn't think you're traveling Top-Star on my credit!"

Hook smiled. "Getting to the bottom of the purse with Welton's, Brett?"

"What do you think? If I don't lay my hands on some of that Vilgene before long—" He broke off. His slanting eyes glistened and then vanished as he slid his eyelids down. All the byplay didn't interest Ryder Hook.

"I'll pay you off, Brett. I'll pay into whatever is the most handy branch of Welton's. But get this through your thick welpac skull. I'm not interested in the Virility Gene. Got it? Count me out."

"Ah, but," said Brett, with his eyes closed. "That's not possible, my illustrious idiot."

Hook didn't bother to reply.

His silence infuriated Brett. The welpac's eyes flew open. "Listen, clunkhead. You owe me. And I'm getting pretty short. There's millions in the Vilgene! Billions! I know the planet and I know the whereabouts and the way of it. I need a partner—"

"Count me out."

"But listen—"

Hook settled the argument by going out and slamming the cabin door.

He went along to the communications center. By this time, if they were still alive, Shaeel and Karg would have reached Jundersborg. He put in a call for them, using the names Balson and Charley, with General Delivery, Jundersborg, and within half an hour the operator called him to say he was through. Hook put the charge down to Brett's account, smirking. It was a trick he thought the welpac would appreciate.

He went into the indicated booth and a screen lit up. The familiar face of Shaeel appeared, and Hook let out a breath of relief. He didn't give a damn for anyone in the galaxy, he kept telling himself; but Shaeel and Karg—well, they were different. Then his face froze with the half-smile all lopsided. This was a recording at which he looked and to which he listened. His face went mean.

"Hi, Abel!" said the pictured recording of the Hermaphrodite. "I trust you're all IQ. Charley and I are. We have a little business to finish with you know who. We're heading out to the Jarhed system—damn rummy place, too, my dear feller, by all accounts." Ve sounded immoderately cheerful. "Very rum. Charley's getting the gear and I'm making this tape for you when you call. As I know you will."

You had to give old Shaeel ves due; ve, too, would never believe Ryder Hook dead until ve had seen him dead with ves own eyeballs.

"And, my Great Hairy Asinine, keep that damned great beak of a Homo sap nose out of trouble, will you, there's a good feller. Oh, by the way, and At No Extra Cost, I bring you a very special greeting. Sharon sends her love."

The screen died.

Shaeel would know very well that there was every chance of ves tape being monitored. Ve'd given nothing away, apart from the solar system to which ve and Karg were going, and ve'd had to do that in order to let Hook know. But what had the Hermaphroditic idiot meant by the last message? Sharon? Hook smiled reflectively. Maybe, just maybe, Shaeel and Karg were out to ask the lovely Tayniss Sharon a few searching questions. Well, if they didn't ask them before Hook did, Hook would have his own questions to ask that scheming bitch.

Before returning to the double second-class cabin to pick up Brett for dinner, for which Brett was going to pay, Hook went along to the ship's library and looked out one or two stellar charts. The illuminated cube lit with the scattered lights, looking, as one famous scribe had said more than once, like a handful of diamonds scattered across a velvet backdrop—and Hook picked out the Jarhed system. H'mm. Just an almost normal F-type sun, with ten planets, three suitable for human habitation. He checked their names.

His mind went racing on with un-Boosted but nevertheless superior-to-normal speed. He'd duck this interesting freak Brett, find a ship passage somehow, get out to the Jahed planets—the names came up on the read-out board.

Rondelle.

Pheruchia.

Shylo.

Ryder Hook flicked the switch and the illuminated cube died. The stellar swarms slaked to ash. He stood up and stretched and felt the old blue coverall distasteful upon him. Well, that would be attended to, also.

He went back to the cabin.

"Where have you been, Hook? It's dinner time."

"This Virility Gene," said Hook. "Seems I might be interested. You want a partner? To do the rough stuff, right?"

"I can do my own rough stuff, Hook. I want a partner to watch my back."

"That sounds an interesting proposition. I'm at a loose end, now, after that nonsense of *Vandeneuf.*"

Hook was not lying. He was always at a loose end in the galaxy, given his unalterable determination to stay alive, unless he was trying to do something exceedingly nasty to the Boosted Men, or looking out for Shaeel. As he was now, he supposed.

Brett stared with calculation writ large upon that alien face. He licked his lips, curving down between those wedge-

45

shaped jaws. He put a hand to his piled hair, reflectively.

"You changed your mind suddenly, Hook. But you're in my debt. You can work it off by bodyguarding me, right?"

"Sure," said Ryder Hook. "It'll be a pleasure."

"And if you try to be too clever, try to switch it on me, I'll do for you, so help me Pakveil."

"You can," said Ryder Hook, "but try—the once."

5

Hook opened his eyes blearily and looked at the metalloy overhead and cursed weakly. Traveling Star-Hard always did make him feel as though he'd been out on a month-long binge and had crawled back to barracks with his tongue trailing in the dust. And some of the antics this non existent month of debauchery had involved him in had included using The Virility Gene. He felt lousy.

He forced himself to lean over the metalloy shelf— there was a mattress but it felt as though it had been stuffed with shrunken Krifmans heads—and glared down at Brett in the lower shelf.

"You out of it yet, Brett?"

Brett said something that Hook could have sworn was: "Ggnnkk uurrk zhush."

"No," said Hook, answering his own question.

In the Star-Hard's passenger cum freight holds the sounds of men and women of a whole range of planetary types waking up sounded like an ancient stockyard before the freight train pulled in. Hook yawned and cocked a leg over the shelf, started to clamber down the ladder. He was stiff and sore, and he ached all over; but he'd arrived safely in one piece. The Hard traveling system was not as flukey as the transmat, effective only over distances that were short inside a galaxy and demanding a loss ratio of one in a million, but it was very exhausting.

Brett rolled over and coughed. His tail showed, fluffy and ragged, most decrepit.

The chief handler strutted down between the aisles of shelves, banging his cane on the struts.

"Get your butts outta there!" he bellowed. "We need to fumigate this place for our next load of stiffs."

He laughed at this joke. Half an hour ago everyone here had been frozen stiff as boards. The air that came pumping in smelled of oil and chemicals. As always after traveling Hard, Hook felt ravenous.

"Roust! Roust!" bawled the chief handler. He wore a fancy green uniform, much adorned with gilt badges, and he carried a holstered gun at his belt. Hook saw the butt, the curve and shape of it, and knew the weapon for a Krifarm model twelve. The chief handler in his snappy uniform was a Krifman, with the high hectoring tone of that arrogant race.

The chief handler's assistants were hard at work emulating their chief. He, in person, came stalking down between the aisles which reared twelve shelves tall. He started yanking people off. Hook saw a young Cailiang girl hauled off by one furry arm. Her tail flapped helplessly. She fell.

"Get up, get up!" shouted the chief. "I ain't got all day."

The girl was clearly still in semishock, not yet fully recovered from the freezing process. Hook felt like a dish rag not quite wrung out. The chief handler strutted on, banging his stick against the metalloy struts, bellowing.

He pushed past Hook, bent and took Brett by the tail. He hauled.

Brett came out, bounced on the floor, and yelled.

His eyes flew open, slanting upward, abruptly evil.

"Hey!" Brett said, offended.

The chief kicked him into action.

"Get up off your butt and get outta here; we've a fresh bunch of gonils coming in. Move it!"

Brett stared up at Hook, who had not moved.

"Duke," said Brett, using the name Hook had adopted to travel Star-Hard to Shyle. "Duke. I'm hiring you to keep gonils like this offa my back."

"Of course," said Hook. "If you pay."

He reached out and knuckled the chief handler. Hook let the smartly uniformed bulk slump to the deck.

"That suit you?"

"It's a start. Wait 'til I get my hands—"

Hook lifted Brett away from the fallen handler.

"You want to get us a bad name, Brett?"

"I just want to pay him back."

"Really! Such violence. It won't do. Come on. Let's get out before the rush."

The byplay had left them caught up with a struggling and confused mass of people all pushing and cursing to get out of that hellhole as fast as possible. Everyone pushed along between the aisles to come out into the lobby and so go streaming out through the metalloy treads of the double-valve airlocks and out into the pale fire of Jarhed. The F type sun swam behind a thin frizzle of cloud. By day it would be hot, here on Shyle, and by night it would be freezing well down from the poles. Hook fancied he would not relish following Brett to the poles. He started around the spacefield. Robot handlers were busily at work bringing the passengers' dunnage out from the Star-Hard. There were no ordinary passengers; he and Brett had booked cheaply, like so many others; the ship had taken her time picking her way here through the interstellar gulfs, calling here for more people to be quick-frozen and stowed away. Many were going on beyond Shyle. Hook noted the queue waiting to board. So people were leaving Shyle, so there were reasons for that, too . . . Interesting.

Customs inspection was strict, and this surprised Hook. He'd been through all manner of customs inspections on plenty of the planets of the galaxy.

Here on Shyle the customs men were of various races, and no one seemed to take any notice of that. There was a race native to Shyle. Brett said so, and he'd paid good money for his information.

Hook gazed around the crowded scene in the customs shed and his thin lips ricked up. It looked as though plenty of other treasure hunters had descended on Shyle. If they were all after Vilgene—what price Brett's secret knowledge?

The same dark thoughts were occurring to the welpac, for he glared about. He did not mutter; but his face showed expressively enough as they passed through customs that he was experiencing the first quivers of doubt—and they inevitably brought an explosion of anger.

Here and there among the crowd other people were thinking exactly the same thoughts as Brett. A number of fights broke out. The customs people moved in and sorted out the trouble; but Hook suspected there was going to be a hot time in the old town tonight. The port at which they had made planetfall was an open spaceport-city. Shyle was a primitive world, endowed with grand and terrifying scenery, and this spaceport-city had been conveniently sited on a delta flatland. In the far distance purple mountains, snow-capped, reared against the flare of Jarhed. The city would be like most other cities, Hook supposed, which simply meant it would be as alienly different as the psychology of its inhabitants and builders dictated.

The surprising item, which made Hook smirk at Brett, was that Shyle remained an Open planet. The econorgs had not yet moved in. Once any kind of thriving industry took root, once there was money to be made, and power to be wielded, then the multi-system conglomerates would send in their men and their machines, and no doubt they'd fight over the planet's resources, and after that would come a stalemate. And then, after that, Shyle would become like any other of the econorg-dominated planets of the galaxy.

Hook, if he'd cared to worry about such things, might have harbored a lingering desire that Shyle could have remained a Free World, that is, a planet that had passed from being Open to a stage where it held, or tried to hold, its own destiny distinct from the econorgs. There were a surprising number of Free Worlds in space; but they were massively outnumbered by those planets on which the various econorgs held the power.

"Roust! Roust! Move along there!"

The customs men were shovelling the people out. The strict examination was clearly intended to turn up items the enforcers here would not wish brought in. Hook took the opportunity to check on what was going through and saw many tracked vehicles, air cushion vehicles, fliers, skimmers, an amazing variety of vehicles designed for the prospecting of difficult country. None was available here, apparently.

Brett had invested almost the last of his credit in a crawler—just about the cheapest form of transport after walking—and digging equipment. He hadn't been able to afford a robot. There were plenty of tinmen about, though, hurrying and scurrying to push their owner's goods through customs.

Burdened with sonic-drill, shovels, food and energy supplies, Hook and Brett climbed aboard their crawler and took off. They had to form in line. As they approached the city from the spaceport they became aware of the sad litter of tumble-down housing shepherded out into the environs, and the lack luster people squatting there. Hook formed an opinion on these people; but he did not confide that opinion to Brett.

There was as great a conglomeration of racial types as Hook had ever seen. This planet of Shyle had attracted people from all over the densely populated portions of the galaxy.

A party of mals preceded Hook and Brett. They had six crawlers and their equipment appeared to consist of a bewildering variety of reaping and threshing machines, huge cumbersome wheels isotopically powered, glittering blades, electronic sorting hoppers, bagging attachments. Brett scowled at them as the procession wound on.

"Hick farmers," he said. He'd bought himself a fresh supply of stim-gum and he chewed with evident satisfaction.

Hook's preternaturally sharp ears picked up what the mals were chattering about. The canopy of the crawler had been opened and despite the general noise and interference of machinery, Hook could hear enough of the mals' conversation to realize without doubt that they, too, were here after The Virility Gene.

He said as much to Brett.

"Naw. No—can't be, Duke. No way."

"That's the impression I receive—and from a lot of other people who made planetfall with us." Hook looked at the derelict huts at the side of the road. People looked up apathetically. "They're all here after The Virility Gene."

"No way, Duke, for them mals." Brett jerked his thumb at the following group of Krifmans who rode a crawler loaded with mining machinery loosely covered by plastic sheeting. "Them Krifmans, maybe. Them mals—never. They don't have mining equipment. Only farming stuff."

Hook wasn't going to tell the welpac about his capacity to eavesdrop when necessary. So Hook contented himself with saying: "You're paying, Brett."

For Ryder Hook, loyalty was a lovely and precious jewel. So rare, this jewel, in the galaxy of the one hundred and first century that Ryder Hook considered you'd never be able to string enough gems together to make a bracelet. He was not a cynical man in the loose and easy way of trite cynicism. He wanted to be—well, that was a maundering daydream. All he could be was what the galaxy would allow, given his gifts. But there were loyalties he treasured; he knew he wouldn't let Shaeel down, if it was humanly possible not to do so. And he fancied Shaeel felt the same way—although you could never tell with such a cutting Hermaphroditic idiot. And Karg, too, had come into the gemmed circuit. There had been Doctor David Chronius, of course, with whom Hook had established a superbly glittering example of the jewel loyalty. But there were precious few others.

"Sure, I'm paying, Duke," said Brett. He was a man of sensibility enough not to bother to add: "And don't you forget it." But the unspoken words lingered in the hot air of Shylo under Jarhed.

The wait to be processed for a prospector's license took longer than anyone there had expected. The heat of the delta lands beat down from the leached sky and upward from the creaking earth. One look at the license office convinced Hook that he'd be wasting his time to fight through. As he said to Brett: "You know the secret of the Vilgene location, right? So why get yourself mussed pushing through all these monkeys? Tomorrow we'll get ourselves a license."

They slept in the crawler cabin that night, and ate their own food. Prices in the hotels and saloons were very high.

The following morning showed almost as large a crowd; but by some chicanery and sleight of hand involving cards played on the hoods of parked vehicles, Brett and Hook worked their way through. Shaeel was a marvel at sharping with the circular cards; Hook was a pretty smart operator with the rectangles of plastic. It took all kinds to make up a galaxy.

The licensing officer—a Homo sap—looked up at them over his desk with pouched eyes, then went back to his records.

"Names?"

53

"Brett Fenris and Duke Everest."

A grunt. A punching of buttons. Then: "General or specific?"

"Ah—" said Brett. "General."

More buttons were punched. "Cash on the table."

"I prefer to use my credit card," said Brett. "It's good—"

"Don't get too many credit cards here, with you bums," said the licensing officer. He made the necessary adjustments and Brett paid. He let that mouth of his droop down for Hook's benefit. Hook guessed the welpac's credit would now be just about completely exhausted with Welton's.

In the normal run of things when a wrist credit card was scanned by the receiver-transmitter at the merchandising outlet the coded pulses would beam to the nearest branch of the econorg concerned, to be checked against credit balances kept daily up-to-date from the central computer. Here, on Shyle, they had no such facilities. Once they had assured themselves that the credit card was genuine and no forgery taped on to the wrist by artificial grafts, the licensing officers must have been instructed to use their own sense and accept the credit worthiness of the presenters. If they ran up too many bad debts the licensing officer would feel the displeasure of the planetary chiefs—the heads of these mysterious inhabitants of Shyle from whom in the normal way The Virility Gene was obtainable.

Hook fancied they must have some stake in this mass invasion, some kind of latter-day gold rush, for they knew only too well the value of Vilgene. From them, the Shyloa, men and women of the galaxy bought The Virility Gene. The secret was closely guarded. So Hook had thought. The murderous business as men fought to obtain that exciting secret had reinforced his view.

But all these people, flooding in, to prospect for Vilgene!

Hook knew the galaxy was a big place, right enough. Here was one more example of just how big the whirlpool of stars really was. No doubt each individual party spacing in here to find Vilgene had bought the secret, paid large sums for it, had gone through hairy adventures as Brett and Hook had done—and here they were by the thousands!

"The quicker we move on, Duke, the better."

"I agree."

Again that nasty business of loyalty obtruded. Brett Fenris was no jewel. But Hook had agreed to keep watching his back.

"Give me an hour, Brett—an hour terrestrial. I've a few inquiries."

"They're dead, Duke. Both of 'em!"

After the hour in which Hook checked the incoming registers via central computer, to come up without a single trace of a Balson or a Charley, a Shaeel or a Karg, he wondered if he should go back and punch Brett's nonexistent welpac nose in for him. He'd definitely put the jinx on this one . . .

Paging the computer for a message via General Delivery proved fruitless. Maybe they were using different names; if so then how in hell did they expect him to guess what they might be? Hook tried half a dozen of the usual aliases they used. Nothing. Perhaps the two clunkheads hadn't arrived, yet. He left a message with General Delivery—collect—saying to Balson and Charley that Abel Klark would be back in town in two months terran. He left a gap between the first and second calls to the computer, and used a different outlet. So that meant he was back to the crawler late.

Brett said: "If I can't trust you to be on time, Duke, how are we gonna get on out in th' badlands?"

"The badlands," said Hook. "I might have known."

"That's just what the locals call it. We'll be snug in the crawler. We'll sink a shaft, grab up enough spoil to prove we've hit a bonanza, and head back here. When we register—ah that'll be the day!"

Again Hook was reminded of the destitutes huddled in their shacks alongside the road.

With the problem of Shaeel not susceptible to solution for the moment, Hook had asked a few questions around. No Hermaphrodite had been seen in a long time. He must push that aside. He had complete confidence in Shaeel's ability to survive the normal perils of the galaxy. If the Boosted Men intervened, why, then Ryder Hook would have to play a different part.

Four times that morning as they arranged air transport out they were approached by different people in different stages of destitution with absolutely guaranteed maps of the true location of The Virility Gene. Brett fidgeted. Hook turned the would-be sellers of billions away. He tried not to be harsh. One old Riffian who had, like so many of his race, a bridge-mounted transducer, looked in a pitiable state. Shrunken arms and legs, gaunt face, all these signs so eloquent on a human were reproduced on the Riffian. His clothes were mere plastic bags lashed with plastic string. He was bare footed.

To this alien ancient Hook handed four peks. He had precious little money metal left.

"Here you are, friend. Get a bowl of soup."

"But the map—"

"Use it to keep warm at night."

The Riffian shuffled off through the dust, his shadow gaunt and black.

Hook knew the value of four peks. It would buy a bowl of nutrient-rich soup from one of the automatic dispensers under their plastic canopies. These vendors were sited in the sleazy part of most cities, piped from central. If you had four peks you could buy a bowl of soup and keep going for about eight hours, terrestrial. They were something in a galaxy where nothing was usually the rule.

Whoever these mysterious people were who claimed Shyle as their ancestral planet, they employed alien labor exclusively, for Hook did not see one around the city, and

56

they kept themselves to themselves. Through their agents they released certain measured amounts of their product on to the market. You could buy shots of The Virility Gene in the galaxy. You had to be wealthy. It was not in plentiful supply. Anyone discovering the source—well, Hook had little faith in the secret Brett had bought with so much trouble for all concerned from the Cailiang Fenton.

Mind you, it would be amusing to find out.

When at last Brett arranged air transport out and their crawler, piled with their luggage, was gravved aboard, Hook was prepared to take the whole expedition a little more seriously. Casting aside all worries over Shaeel, he determined to do what he had been hired for; as a loyal workman he would earn his wages, and if, at the end, there was this fabulous treasure of The Virility Gene—well, by dear old Dirty Bertie Bashti's underpants, he'd dig in there, too...

Brett did what was expected and had the hired pilot put them down two hundred kilometers from wherever it was he thought the secret lay. The ground came up a dun ochre. There was precious little moisture here, well south of this massive continent of Shyle, past the tall mountains, down into the badlands. Dust puffed. The wind blew dry. The pilot was so matter-of-fact Hook guessed he had delivered treasure seekers out into the wilds before, and had probably never seen them again.

"All set?" he called down from the cabin. "This is no place for a human being."

He was a dark prosaic man from Anselm, armor-plated.

"We won't be here long, fren," called back Brett. He rubbed his hands. Already his massive coif of hair was thick with blown dust. He laughed. "We'll be back, don't you fret."

"I won't."

"The flier took off. They were alone in the badlands, alone with heat and dust and death.

6

Brett Fenris was doing all right until he broke his little finger, then if he'd had a nurse handy he would have wept on her breast.

"But it damn well *hurts*, Hook!"

"Take it easy. Anyway, I told you to stand clear when the drill came up."

"Pakveil take the confounded thing."

The camp had been established where Brett said the secret was to be found. They had trekked in the crawler into the lower foothills, as eroded and dry as the badlands themselves, merely a harsh and unlovely part of the badlands. Ochre and orange rock crumbled at a touch. Boulders tumbled about them during the day as wind and sun—that F-type Jarhed above—leached away their footings. By night a cold wind razored across the badlands, further eroding the rocks. By day the dust choked everything. By night the cold froze everything.

"This must have been like the first guys on Mars experienced," said Hook. "Except we can breathe the air."

"Mars?" said Brett. He nursed his finger and swore from time to time with great conviction. "Where in hell's that?"

"Oh, those old-timers wouldn't recognize it now. It's been terraformed. Quite nice, now, if you like that kind of thing."

"Well, I like nothing, now, Hook. Nothing!"

Hook splinted the finger up and gave Brett a soothing drug and told him to care for his little finger for he fussed as if he'd broken his best leg.

The camp presented a spectacle of hard work. That had the power to depress Ryder Hook. He was not work shy; far from it. But, somehow, he was more and more convinced that this work would go for nothing. The secret Brett had bought from Fenton was worthless. The drill had gone down and brought up ochre sand and dust and orange sand and dust and one day, to great excitement, brought up a trace of a layer of black residue. On examination this turned out to be the remains of perhaps a million years of geologic evolution when this area had been under water. As far as any trace of what Brett was looking for was concerned; nothing came up the whining drill.

The mountains curved away east and west. The sun shone. The dust blew. The nights were bitterly cold. They lived in the crawler's cabin, and they worked the drill, and Brett broke his little finger and cursed. Hook decided that he would have to break the news to Brett—news he felt convinced the welpac was already well aware of and would not admit into his consciousness.

"I don't know what exactly whatever it is we're looking for looks like—"

"Neither need you! That's my business."

Hook could be patient when he chose.

"But wherever it is they get The Virility Gene from—I'd say it's not here."

"We've only gone down twenty taps so far. There's a lot more—"

"How big an area did Fenton say to cover?"

"He wasn't too specific." Brett spoke sulkily. His finger

throbbed despite medication. "I need a drink. Then we'll sink a new bore."

Privately Hook considered he knew who was the bore around here. They'd done a bore morning and afternoon for ten days. Shyle's days were somewhat shorter than Earth's. He considered. Give Brett a full fifty bores. All right. Fifty bores. After that—fini.

"Perhaps we should go deeper?"

"Fenton said at the hundred meter mark would do."

"I'll take this one down two hundred."

"That's wasting time."

"Two hundred."

At two hundred metres they came across further evidence of the vast and slow geological changes that had affected this area. Evolution proceeded on almost all planets in ways comprehensible to terrestrials with the experience of old Earth to guide them. Shells and oil—oil in no quickly usable form—and oil promise could not halt men searching for The Virility Gene. They withdrew the drill and Brett swore as he saw the sonic-laser bit.

"We have only one spare—and if you go down two hundred meters again you'll ruin that, too."

Hook didn't care if they shoved in a knife and fork. He had promised Brett. That, and that alone, kept him working.

A flier slanted against the sun, circled twice, and then let down for a landing.

Brett had not grumbled when Hook had insisted they buy side arms as part of their equipment. Hook knew better than to advise any galaxy wanderer about the best kind of weapon to use. Brett's money had gone on two Tonota Forty hand guns, the best they could afford. Now Hook eased his gun in its holster as the flier came in.

Three men and a girl stepped out, stretching, already blinking as the dust hit them before they slapped filters across their helmets. Hook's hand rested on the butt of his gun. Brett already had his weapon out, handling it awkwardly with his left hand, his right little finger splinted.

"Damned little finger," he growled.

The leader of the approaching group held up a hand and called out.

"Hi, frens! No problems. Saw your site and dropped in for a chat." He spread his hands wide. Hook watched without speaking. He could see the gun at the man's waist.

The four of them came nearer. They were Homo sapiens.

"We'll talk," said Brett. "But we can take you."

After ten minutes wary conversation, Hook came to the conclusion these people were prospectors who, if they were not attacked, would be harmless. Drinks were handed out

The leader, a man with a black beard and a glinting smile, drank and wiped the back of his hand across his lips.

"You've got it easy here, frens."

"Easy!" yelped Brett.

"Yes. We've been to the south. Real bad. Given in. I can tell you, I don't like it. But my girl here has the truth of it. We were fooled. There's no Vilgene around here."

"*You* say so."

One of the other men laughed, a little too shrilly. Hook saw that all these people were fine drawn, on the edge of nervous exhaustion. "You can dig as long as you like, dig till the head freezes over. The Shylao know where the Vilgene is. They're not telling anyone, specially the likes of us."

The man's eyes looked pointedly at Brett's gun. The welpac put the gun down on the drill casing.

"Not the gun, fren. That's IQ. You don't know us. No—I mean your credit card."

"So?"

"So most of us prospectors are loners. We don't have a credit card between us."

"Most of the prospectors like that?"

"Sure. When the econorgs come ablasting in, there's going to be big trouble."

"They'll come," said Hook. "You can count on it."

"They might," said the bearded man, nastily. "They won't find any more Vilgene than we have."

Hook knew the man wasn't questioning what he said. His semantic way of putting it meant that if the econorgs did come in—as they must inevitably do—they would be met with opposition.

The conversation went on for a space and then the party said they must push on. The bearded man, who said his name was Cregson, seemed to Hook trustworthy enough. A man who had paid out for lying information. Brett watched them go and then came back to Hook and glared at him.

"Fenton never sold me a pup."

"We'll dig and find out."

"Yes. We'll do that."

Hook spaced out the fifty drill holes. Brett shouted petulantly when he went up into the foothills, and so Hook gathered that Fenton's much-vaunted information ruled out that area. The days came and went and the area was covered. Hook had reached forty five borings when Brett came over that night to the drill, where Hook was carrying out much-needed maintenance. The welpac looked tired.

"It's no good, Hook. That bastard Fenton cheated me. If I catch up with him I'll—"

"It's too easy to lose yourself in the galaxy, Brett."

"So they say. If you can't read a star chart, that is."

"Check." Any catalogue of stars would give their types and characteristics. You could construct a location-sphere with the star you wanted at the center. But you had to know the stellar populations of the location sphere, as well as that of the target to do that. You could so get lost in the whirlpool of stars.

That old nightmare of Hook's, where he was down on a planet where they did not have interstellar travel and so was forever cut off from the pulsing life in the whirlpool of stars, seemed to him only marginally more horrible than the story he had heard of this man who had got himself lost in the galaxy. Hook seldom felt sorry for anyone, but he could allow he felt profoundly sorry for any clunkhead who got himself lost among the stars.

"Even so," said Brett Fenris, rubbing his tail with his left hand. "Even so, one day I'll catch up with the bastard."

"This means you admit you were conned?"

Brett clearly was most reluctant to admit this. But the evidence was too strong.

"So I was cheated, so all right. But this is the planet where The Virility Gene comes from," He gestured widely. "It's got to be around here, somewhere!"

"Come on!" said Hook. "A planet's a big place."

"So it's big! So we'll find out where these gonils of Shylao hang out."

"Yes," said Ryder Hook, considering. "Yes. That might prove interesting—and rewarding."

Brett's calm acceptance of what had happened might have puzzled Hook had he not realized the broken little finger played a big part in that tranquility. One day, soon, Brett was going to break out and bust loose. Hook wondered if he ought to hang around to witness what might prove amusing.

That night their local alarms cheeped.

Brett sat up in the darkened crawler cabin.

"You hear that, Hook?"

"I hear. There's a prowler outside."

"It's that gonil Cregson come back. He was too smooth."

Hook hoped it wasn't. He'd read Cregson as a man tired and old and wanting to get out of a situation he should never have been in in the first instance.

He eased off the bunk, slid the Tonota into his fist,

padded to the door. He checked the telltales. Brett came up and breathed in his ear.

"There! Three of 'em!"

The scope showed three iridescent figures moving toward the crawler from the direction of the hills. The figures, unidentifiable on the low-power telltale—low-power because low-cost—spread out. This was a definite raid. Hook knew the signs. This must be a party of prospectors who had had no luck themselves, and who were moving in on the new boys. He still did not think Cregson had any hand in this.

"This is what I hired you for, Hook!"

"So I'll earn my keep. You stay here. Don't blast unless you know it's not me—got it?"

"You going outside? Man—they'll fry you."

Hook didn't answer.

The door eased open, dark within and dark without, he felt he would remain unseen at this distance; but there was no time to hang around arguing. He hit the sand without a sound and moved rapidly to his left, silently, like a ghost; and, if asked, like a ghost with very evil intentions.

There was every chance the three would-be choppermen creeping up on him carried sophisticated detector equipment of their own. Body emission detectors would be of little value at this range. They'd have advanced radar, sonics, uv's and suchlike, all of which were guaranteed to pick a target out of the ground clutter at ranges increasing with the credit expended. Hook possessed in his skull, along with those organic implants that enabled him to call out across the parsecs a dinky little homotropic fouler-upper. He had once said the equipment had been installed by a certain Filker Fredericks. They had not been, of course, being there in his head by courtesy of EAS; but old Filker would have been proud to have been thus honored. Hook felt some confidence that the three assassins—although that was far too pungent a word for these three—wouldn't pick him up.

He carried a resonating crystal in his pocket so that his iridescent image would appear on the telltale in the crawler; but that was strictly old-fashioned cheap equipment.

If these three had exactly the same equipment, operating on exactly the same wave cycles—then they'd see Hook, also, and fry him.

He moved cautiously, right hand extended, moving out, keeping low. He was effectively protected from highly sophisticated homotropic devices; a crude radar might pick him out against the clutter, a kicked stone would sound loudly in the breathing night, a footfall slithering on a loose patch of dust would betray him. He walked like a shadow.

Star-glitter fell about him and already his eyes were picking up the shadowed bulk of the crawler, the stark angles of the drill, the piles of gear stacked to one side. He could see the hazy vanishing point of the stars way up where the mountains blocked the light. He could see no intruders. But they were there.

Ryder Hook used his ears.

The soft sibilance of breathing controlled and muffled reached him from his right. He listened out ahead. A scuffle of dust, a slither—sounds that would betray him now betraying the would-be murderers. He listened to the left and heard nothing. One at a time—but he did not care to move until he had pinpointed the number three.

He listened more carefully now, hearing the subtle scurry of the night breeze, the patter of disturbed dust, calculating that was windblown and not foot-kicked. Where the hell was the third gonil?

The two he had pinpointed came on, stealthily. Hook waited. He still could not pick up the third, out to his left. He ought to have gone that way. But out of right or left, you had a fifty-fifty chance. Ryder Hook seemed to have picked the wrong one.

At last he could wait no longer. They'd be opening up

65

pretty soon, and although the crawler was sketchily armored and would resist some energy blasting, it wouldn't last long. And Brett would complain most bitterly. Hook almost let the curds out there start firing at the thought.

Then he went after the intruder to the right. He came up very close, so that the man's breathing sounded close and harsh, even though normal ears could not have heard him outside three meters. Hook let the Tonota droop. He flicked the dis-gel gun into his hand, shot into the darkness aiming directly on the center of the breathing sounds.

The moment he fired he flattened to the ground and listened out for the center man.

The right-hand man screamed.

Hook knew what was happening to him now. Well, the curd shouldn't have crept up like a chopperman. Hook did not think he'd come as a friendly neighbor to borrow a cup of sugar.

The center man rasped a cutting whisper through the night.

"What is it, Dell?"

Dell couldn't answer. His screams choked off. By now he would be knee high, and melting all the time, deliquescing into a slimy pool, vanishing.

The dis-gel gun wouldn't reach to the center man.

Hook moved forward carefully. If he fired the Tonota the unheard would-be murderer over on the left would spot the point of discharge, and fire, and so—exit Ryder Hook.

"Dell?"

The center man must be coming to the conclusion that the noise Dell had made, and his own shouts, must have awakened the occupants of the crawler. Hook fancied the guy would shoot at the crawler, anyway, just to make sure. Hook had no real feelings for Brett Fenris; sure, the welpać was a cheerful clunkhead to have around, and he had broken his little finger. Hook sighed. He didn't relish these intricacies in a simple little shootout.

He listened out to the center man, pinpointed him—absolute exactness would not be necessary for he had the Tonota set on fan with enough power to do the job at this wide aperture setting—and set the gun down on the ground pointing in the right direction. He clipped the length of twine from his boot on to the trigger, backed off unreeling as he went. When he was what he considered a safe enough distance back from the gun, and with the center man still not having made up his mind to shoot—Hook pulled the string.

He didn't look at the gun, he didn't look where the center man was, he didn't look where the blast went. He looked out to where the one on the left should be.

The glare lit up the landscape.

Instantly an answering blast came in from the left.

The jagged power of the weapon near-blinded Hook. He blinked, got its center oriented in his mental picture of the site, with the crawler as locus, and started off crawling.

He didn't bother to collect the Tonota. Its metal parts proof against its own energy would be all right—the butt and the other bits and pieces would be charred scrap.

That invader up there had fired a Martian Mega. That was a very powerful hand gun.

Hook heard the rumbling trembling through the air. He heard the tired sussuration of the air rushing past. He squinted up against the stars. It seemed to him the whole mountain was on the move.

The blasts hadn't done it. Aeons of wind and rain and sun had eroded the mountain top, leaving it all set to topple. The blasts had merely released the trigger.

The mountain top slid down, roaring and thundering in the night, creating a frightening avalanche, pouring down through the darkness, spouting in dusty power that blotted out the stars. All that massive power, those millions of tons of rock, roared down and rolled out toward the crawler, to Brett Fenris in the crawler, to a would-be assassin outside—and to Ryder Hook.

7

The mountain fell.

Rocks and stones and tumbling boulders crashed past Hook. He dived flat into a shallow gulley. Dust billowed down, choking him, unseen in the shifting darkness. The noise bellowed insanely and he blanked off ninety per cent of that incredible hearing ability. He endured. The ground shook, cracks appeared in the dusty soil, rock outcrops thrust through like fangs. The mountain went on falling, streaming like an insanely speeded-up glacier of stone across the badlands, engulfing everything in its path.

After a time Hook heard the noise levels recede. His ears ached and his head rang. He brushed clinging sand and dust from his body and struggled to stand. The gully had given him enough protection. The dust streaked away beneath the stars, pale and almost luminous, fanning out beyond the gully like a dry wash.

The crawler had been battered, upended, overturned, flung headlong. A rind of moon cast shards of weird light down through the hanging dust. Hook blinked. He struggled out of the clinging debris and then relaxed on the edge of the gully. He spent some time just looking out. He had every expectation that the one on the left had survived, too. Until he had either assured himself the chopperman was dead or had dealt with him, he would not—could not—hurry across to the crawler. Brett Fenris must wait.

A shadow moved beneath that rind of moon. Hook watched. A dark figure crawled cautiously across the dust toward the crawler. Presently the figure elongated, darkened, took shape. The man was investigating the crawler. Now, if at all, was the time for Brett to cut loose with his Tonota.

Hook began to worm his way across the dust. The ground resembled the aftermath of a battle. Rocks tumbled from the fallen mountain gave him cover. He went with some speed. He made no sound.

Now the figure was moving more carefully still around to the far side of the overturned crawler. Hook did not risk any lifting of his body to go faster, no raising of himself to greater visibility; but he put on speed. He went faster than he would have done had the chopperman been in sight.

By the time the figure emerged from the far side of the crawler, having inspected all sides, and Hook sank down again into the dust in the lee of a rock, Hook had gained a vantage point from which to shoot. The dis-gel gun would just reach.

There was no hesitation about Ryder Hook in these matters.

The moon now gave enough light for him to know he would not miss.

Ryder Hook did not believe in missing when he shot.

He watched as the would-be murderer died. Hook did not jump and run forward. He had seen a man dying from the deliquescing effects of dis-gel rush with an axe upon his killer and slay him. Such incredible fortitude did not amaze Hook; it made him cautious

When the third of the trio of would-be assassins had

vanished Hook went across. He saw the Martian Mega lying on the sand. Later, with great care, he would clean it and strap it to his own waist to replace the lost Tonota. He had made a most advantageous deal. He pushed the door of the crawler open and shouted.

"You all right, Brett?"

A hoarse and dust-clogged voice husked: "All right, you great clunkhead! I've just about broken every bone in my body and my tail's all torn."

Hook did not smile. He went into the upturned cabin and rooted around and felt Brett and made sure his alien anatomy was all in one piece. He plastered the torn tail and gave the welpac a shot. Then he sat back and said:

"The three who did this must think you have the secret, still, Brett. But I do not think so. I think it's time we moved out."

They spent most of the rest of the night arguing. By the time the sun, that F-type Jarhed, rose over the badlands, Brett had agreed to leave this very morning.

"No point in wasting any more time. That bastard Cailiang sold me a pup."

"Maybe he didn't know, one or the other, either."

"Yes," said Brett as he watched Hook preparing breakfast. "That must have been it. He had a good story. Couldn't go himself because of his poor ailing mother. That's why he was willing to sell the secret. Make a little money that way." Brett sat up, sharply. "Not so much salt in the damned egg pudding, Hook! Anyway," he went on, fretfully. "The other bastards—Sharon and Rhus and Carshder—couldn't have got to him—unless—"

Hook waited as the awful idea percolated through to Brett's appalled brain.

"Oh, no!" said the welpac. "No! I don't believe it."

Hook handed the welpac his egg pudding, a delicacy for breakfast, apparently, on Lemphale.

70

"No, don't believe it, Brett. In my view Fenton sold you all false information. He would have varied the supposed site of Vilgene so as to prevent you all meeting up. He's off somewhere, now, in the whirlpool of stars, spending all your money and laughing fit to bust a gut."

"I'll bust more than a gut if I catch up with him."

"Don't fret. Put it down to experience."

"You're a cold-blooded curd, aren't you?"

"When it is necessary."

After Brett had eaten his breakfast, and Hook had swallowed down some reconstituted bacon and egg, Brett said:

"So how do we get out of here? The crawler's busted, the radio's smashed. Walk?"

"You didn't break your leg, only your little finger, you can walk."

"You'll have to carry me. I'm worn out."

Hook didn't intend to carry the welpac out. He did not much fancy walking out alone, either.

The dishwasher was not working after the battering the crawler had taken, and Hook tossed the plastic plates down before Brett.

"You clean these up. I'll be gone for I don't know how long. I'll be back before dark, though."

"You're leaving me, Hook! You gonil! You're running out!"

The Tonota clicked from Brett's holster. Hook had more than half-expected this reaction. It was perfectly natural. He chopped down, knocked the gun away.

"I'm not leaving you, you iridium-plated idiot! I'll be back before it's dark. And don't shoot before you know it's not me."

"Yeah—" Brett glared up, angry, frustrated, paining. "And when I do know it's you I might still shoot."

Hook laughed at this. A good belly laugh.

"You want to commit suicide, laddie, that's up to you."

"You think you're so smart—"

"No," said Ryder Hook, very seriously, his face abruptly sombre. "I'm not smart enough. But I try to be careful."

"Well, where by Pavkeil are you going?"

Hook sighed. He might have said: "If you haven't the sense to figure that out you've no real right pretending to be a galactic adventurer." Instead, he said: "You'll see when I get back. If I draw a blank, you won't be disappointed."

Brett picked up his Tonota. He hefted it. "If I didn't believe in you, Hook, I'd have used the Delling. You knew that."

"I knew."

"Well, for the sake of Pakveil—bring it back!"

Hook jumped from the crawler. So old Brett had sussed it out. There was hope for the welpac yet in this unfriendly and hostile galaxy.

Hook's famous old black boots took him swiftly through the dust. He headed for the foothills. With all the instrumentation of the crawler shattered, and without wishing to spare the time it would take to lash up a detector board, Hook intended to rely on eyesight and intuition. Now where would he have set down up in these hills?

In the event he found the would-be assassins' fliers in a gully, more or less on a direct line from where the site had been laid out. He scouted the place cautiously. If the three dead men had been Cregson and his comrades, the girl would still be in the flier. When he got a clear look at the craft Hook knew his instincts had been right. This was a different model.

He spent some time watching, and finally convinced himself the flier was empty. All the same he stalked in with a very great care.

He had been pretty sure they'd come in a flier. A crawler would have been buried underneath the rubble of the fallen mountain. As it was, a slide of loose stones and rocks had pitched down so close that one of the fliers unnecessary but sporty rear fins had been bent. He opened the door and shouted:

"Hey! Anyone at home! I need help."

But his precautions were in vain. The flier was empty, and quick inspection showed the occupants to have been three men, probably Homo mal by the toiletry. He chucked these out, ventilated the craft, checked the engines, and then took her up in a rather liberal swirl of power, flattened out and so dived down to land next to the crawler.

He stepped out and, for an instant, wondered if a bolt of energy from the welpac would incinerate him.

Instead Brett called out: "Nice going, Hook."

"Just remember it's Duke Everest when we meet people."

They took what was salvageable and left the junk.

They wasted no time in getting airborne and heading back to the nearest tavern where a drink and some information might be had. As Brett said: "We'll give the spaceport a miss. Let's nose around out here for a spell."

Hook had said two months. There was time.

"IQ, Brett."

There were very many areas of Shyle to be considered. The flier Brett had acquired—for, of course, by the terms of their contract, the flier was his—could swish them around the planet in short order. In the ensuing days they roamed at will, the nuclear engines fueled for the next fifty years, terrestrial, their food just about adequate, what with their own and what was in the flier. They heard rumor and counter rumor. Many times they encountered groups of disillusioned prospectors, and they had to fight only once. More and more prospectors were coming to realize that no one possessed the secret. They passed abandoned sites and rusting machinery. Some men were absolutely convinced the secret of Vilgene was to be found in a certain plant. Hook saw hundreds of plants brought into the frontier towns to be tested and tossed aside. Other men knew for certain Vilgene was obtained from animals, and the slaughter went on, to no avail.

The tenseness of men showed itself in strange ways. Hook began to feel he could ease off the watchfulness, for one disappointed seeker-after Vilgene recognized another, a man whose dearly bought secret had proven false recognized another man in the same situation. There were newcomers, as Brett and Hook had been, who might cause trouble. But the aura of puzzled despair that hung over Shyle soon gripped them. Those who could not cope with the conditions finished up in the hopeless shacks lining the road to the spaceport.

"The gall of these Shylao!" said Carl, in one of the frontier taverns where prospectors congregated. "They just don't care about the picture those poor devils make. You'd think they'd want to clear 'em away for fear of frightening off new arrivals."

"No," said Tendris, wiping beer suds from his mostache. "It's the enforcers they use. The Shylao just keep their hooks on the Vilgene and the money."

"Aye, that's right!"

"I'd like to—"

"Bastard Shylao!"

Hook and Brett propped the bar up and listened. Despite his own cocky ways, Brett had unconsciously absorbed some of Hook's quiet philosophy of staying out of trouble. For his part Hook had been asking and listening, not for The Virility Gene's true whereabouts, but for his two comrades, Shaeel and Karg. He had discovered nothing, and he intended to return to the spaceport where they had landed exactly as the two stipulated months expired.

Like most of the people here, Hook and Brett had scraped enough money by selling their equipment to those who were settling here. In addition Hook had manipulated the cards in ways that would have given Shaeel goose pimples, and made a little money-metal.

This place was wide-open, raucous, vile and violent, and it was only one among thousands. Rumors spread like prairie fires. People coming in were avidly questioned and as soon as it became clear—as it did every time—that they had been as unsuccessful as every one else in their quest, interest in them waned and they could merge into the background.

Perhaps the strangest thing of all to Ryder Hook was the feeling that as a loner, a man without a credit card and an allegiance to an econorg, he was not the sore thumb here. Those with credit cards were the sore thumbs. Brett kept his sleeve well pulled down.

Science and all the marvels of technology were spreading over this planet of Shyle. The Shylao were selling the Virility Gene and were being paid fortunes. The stuff could be obtained in tablet form, or as an injection, and it worked. That it worked was proved indisputably by all the voracious seekers after Vilgene treasure gathered here.

"Then," said Carl, getting at Tendris, "why'd the Shylao let us in? Why risk us finding Vilgene?"

"That's easy," pointed out a mal, who looked half-starved. "If they tried to shut us out the econorgs would move in just because that's their style. Any planet tries to shut people out gets turned over, you'll know that. But if the Shylao take no notice—let everyone in, why, the econorgs must figure there's nothing to it."

"They'll be here, soon. The Shylao must know that. It's only a matter of time."

"The galaxy's a big place, clunkhead. It'll take time."

"But it will happen. And my guess—" and here Carl glared most ferociously. "My guess is it's going to be soon!"

A troupe of girls who earned enough to live on danced in then and the men gave them their attention, shouting, whistling, clapping. The girls danced reasonably well; but Hook had no interest in them. His eyes kept flicking across the smokey tavern with its close smells of beer and wine, redolent of the vices of the galaxy, to a corner booth. Here sat a dynaman—rather, he rested on the smooth lower portions of his metalloy carapace. His tentacular arms could lift his glass of liquor, and he could down it with evident relish. He had been a Krifman, before his voluntary amputations had given him the chance to inhabit the well-nigh indestructible metalloy shell of a dynaman. Now he laughed and joked with a couple of mal girls, and they were teasing him into buying more liquor.

Brett said: "What's so all-fired important about the dynaman, Duke?"

"He's getting above himself, Brett. He was listening to Carl and Tendris arguing, and I swear he knows something about the Shylao that—"

"That we should know!" Brett was by now fully satisfied that if Ryder Hook, alias Duke Everest, said something, that something was so.

Brett's short squab tail jerked into rigid determination. He straightened his wide shoulders and started off for the corner booth and the dynaman. Hook caught his arm and hauled him back.

"What th' hell's up with you, Ho—Duke?"

"Knock it off, Brett! Handle the dynaman with care. In that force-field cocoon he's got power-weapons, all kinds, you name it—you want your guts blown out through your backbone?"

"If you put it like that..."

"Fetch a fresh bottle 'o that rot gut he's drinking—"

"That's local-brewed four-comet! It'll cost—"

"Bring it!"

Brett punched the buttons and the bar vender slapped out its circular scoop with the four-comet bottle all new and fresh and frosty. It had come up from the vats of pure in the cellars, had additives sprinkled in, given the treatment, had a good three minutes to mature. It was good stuff. Hook shoved Brett on and, with the bottle, and with fatuous smiles plastered on their ugly faces, they wandered over to the dynaman.

Hook used a most subtle approach.

"Hey, dynaman!" he said, letting his body sway an artistic fraction. "Old Rocco told me you know the real place! He said you had the real true on-the-line information. Wanna buy it offa yuh—we gotta deal?"

He sat down, keeping his thin lips stretched into that asinine smile, nudged the naked thigh of one of the girls. She simpered, sensing custom. Hook slammed the bottle of four-comet on the booth table. "Drink up, frens! There's more where that came from."

With a chilling efficiency the dynaman's heavy duty grabs lifted the bottle. One held the bottle, the other twisted off the cap with a shirring splintering of glass. His tentacles positioned his glass and he poured out two drinks. With the same fluidity of motion he poured two more. His eyes that had once been Krifman eyes regarded Hook with a thin glitter.

"Your health, sap."

Hook could take that. Homo sapiens. Well, if you were Homo mal, or a Krifman, or any other of the races of the galaxy, what would you call a Homo sapiens?

"Drink up, sap!"

"Oh, Selkas!" giggled one of the girls.

"Here," said Brett, suddenly flushed of face. "That ain't a polite thing to call a Homo sapiens, dynaman, and damn well you know it!" Then, at the dynaman's abrupt and evil flash from upturned eyes, Brett swallowed and went on with what he was saying and making it into a laugh, a throw away line: "Why, even I wouldn't call the clunkhead that!"

Hook had observed the quality of the dynaman's cocoon. It was high grade. It was guaranteed to withstand quite a considerable amount of energy, and would stop a Tonota forty, say, completely. Hook did not think it capable of withstanding a Martian Mega for more than five or six minutes. Of course, by then, unarmored as he was, he'd have been cut down by the dynaman's cocoon-mounted weapons.

"It's IQ," said Hook. "Sure! Les' all drink up!"

By acting as the genial and half-imbecile drunk who would believe that a dynaman on Shyle would both know the whereabouts of the Vilgene and sell the secret to him, Hook passed the evening in pleasant drinking and talk, always harping on the secret. "That ol' Viri'lty Gene's gotta be somewhere's around here. Just gotta be!" And by the time the moon floated free—Shyle possessed one visible moon and four invisible from the surface—Hook felt he had wormed his way rather well into the good books of the dynaman Selkas.

The raw liquor they were pouring down Selkas's throat helped. He might have a force-field cocoon and a metalloy carapace around him, he might have two sinuous tentacles and two heavy duty grabs, he might have an artificial gravity unit for locomotion; but he still had the metabolism of a man and a human Krifman stomach. Hook got the dynaman far more than half-brensschluss. And that damned welpac idiot Brett was silly-happy, too. The two girls were sprawled on the table, heads on arms, out to the world.

"Yeah, Duke," giggled Brett. "I don't reckon ol' Selkas here has any better idea nor what we have—"

"You ignorant welpac clunky," said Selkas, and he burped—an interesting phenomenon, that, within the cocoon. "Carshder's gonna fix it all up. You take it from me."

Brett glanced at Hook and opened his mouth, and Hook said: "You pull the other one, Selkas. An' don' forget—I've got two legs to pull, not like some people I know."

Selkas flared up. He was going to pass out any minute, and again Brett opened his mouth. This time Hook kicked him under the table. One of the girls yelped in her sleep, and

Brett closed his mouth. If he hadn't received the kick he'd received the message. And Selkas was hugely and drunkenly annoyed they wouldn't believe him.

"There's no secret, you clunkheads. Carshder's got the right idea. He's checked the Shylao out—he'll be back soon, some time, an' then—and' then—"

The dynaman's head could not fall far within the force field. But it drooped as far as it would go.

Hook stood up, swaying still, in case interested eyes watched. He was about to bawl Brett out for getting half-drunk when a sudden and unnatural silence in the tavern brought horror.

8

Carshder walked into the tavern at midnight, still tall, still a Krifman, but incredibly thin, filthy, slashed with a thousand razor cuts, and two black hoofmarks for eyes.

The horror of his appearance as he stood there, swaying eerily, his gash of a mouth tight-lipped with inner terror, drove a chill of unease through the room.

A stink hung about him, the grave-dirt smell gone rotten, redolent of a million slimy gutters, fetid vampire suckings, sweet and sickly scents of operating tables in the mud and blood of the trenches, the unmistakable retching aroma of putrid flesh.

The silence in the tavern hung like a ripped blanket of night over a violated tomb.

No woman screamed, no man raised his glass. The fearsome thing that was this crucified Krifman held them all in thrall.

Carshder was falling to pieces as he walked. His arms and legs jutted with the stiffness of pistons. He walked as though jointed with bent wires. Slowly he tottered toward the corner table in the booth where the dynaman Selkas lay with his massive head down-drooping, out to the side.

Hook stood up.

"Hey, Carshder!" he bellowed, so that glasses chimed and women let out squeaks of surprise and men jumped. "Hey! C'm over here and have a drink! You look fair tuckered out."

"The Shylao!" whispered a husky looking man, very green under the jaw, his eyes wide.

"The Shylao!" ran the whisper around the tavern.

On tottered the wreck of Carshder. His skin was peeling back from those thousands of tiny razor cuts. His face showed hair-fine lines of red, pulsing, dribbling thin trickles of blood. As he walked he left a trail of bloody footprints. His body was slowly falling to pieces. How far he had walked like that Hook would not like to guess.

But Hook could guess what had happened to the poor devil. The Shylao—if this was their handiwork—had exposed him to similar effects to those obtained by dis-gel, so that his body was deliquescing—but it was taking a long time to melt. The torture through which Carshder was going must inevitably have made him mad.

Hook shouted again. "Carshder, you old space dog! Come on, fren. Siddown and have a splash."

A woman screamed, now, and a man seized her arm and fairly dragged her from the tavern. Glasses went smash on the floor. Men and women of many different races made for the door in a panicky rush. Brett stood up, alongside Hook.

"Don't let him touch me!"

"I wouldn't take even money he won't fall to pieces before he reaches this booth."

"You're a cold-blooded devil, Hook!"

"You've said that before. And if you forget I'm Duke Everest I'll knock your teeth down your throat."

Hook did not believe in threats. If it had to be done—do it. But in this case he felt a little timely reminder might prevent the doing of what he promised.

"Sure, sure, Duke."

Carshder's sinews were failing him now so that his arms and legs dangled. He could not move on. He was held up only by the locking of his knee and hip bones. Then they, too, sloughed. Carshder fell. He fell face down, full length, like a tree. Hook stood looking down on him.

There was a great deal he could have said. But it all would have been superfluous oratory, copy-book stuff of academe. The reality was here and now. Men lived and men died. That was all.

Brett was recovering now the immediate threat had passed.

"We'd better get out of here, Ho—Duke."

"We can't leave Selkas. He might be useful."

"And the girls?"

Hook was a real right bastard in the galaxy, he knew that; but, now, the obvious course might not be the right one. "You drag 'em out. I'll see to fren Selkas."

Brett grabbed the two girls and began dragging them away. He gave the corpse a wide berth. The skeleton showed through now as the skin and flesh dripped through. Hook took out the Martian Mega, unscrewed the service plate, connected up two jumper wires from his boot. He placed the wires against the dynaman's metalloy cocoon. He had to choose his spot with care, just where a rivetted area beneath the skin gave access, for naturally the cocoon was non-conducting. Hook fancied he had the area about right. He gave a tiny squirt of juice. Nothing happened. Hook increased the amperage, and slowly moved the terminals about the area he fancied—there! Selkas's eyelids jumped. Hook pumped up the power, gave a tickle that would have fried a nice rasher of reconstituted bacon, and made the dynaman's head snap upright and his eyelids fly up and his mouth open and: "What the hell's going on! Ow! That hurt!"

"Get your anti-gravs working, Selkas."

"What—?"

"Look there! That's what's left of your pal Carshder."

Selkas looked. The sight appeared to have no effect on him at all. But then, all he could see were tattered clothing, a skull falling in like a morning boiled eggshell, and a twist of thigh bones jutting from a collapsing pelvis.

"Let's get out of here, Selkas. If the Shylao did that to Carshder, they might come looking for the guy who sent him."

"They won't do that, Duke," said the dynaman. But he popped a kill-'em pill into his mouth, swallowed and followed Hook to the door smartly. "They protect their secrets. They don't interfere outside their own preserves."

"You must tell me. I could be interested."

Selkas the dynaman hummed smoothly across the tavern towards the door, travelling a meter above the floor. He passed directly over the remnants of Carshder and he did not stop or look down. Instead he said: "You mean that, Duke? If so, I could be of use to you."

"And you expect me to be of use to you—and I might wind up like Carshder here?"

"I read you for a resourceful man."

They were outside under the moon, with the heavy memory of the Krifman Carshder between them.

"I like the odds on my side when I take chances. And I don't like taking chances anyway."

"No risk, Duke. Carshder made a mess of it."

Brett and the girls were across the street, silent and dim now. "Those girls," said Hook. "They're your responsibility. Brett and I are sleeping in our flier."

"Walk to my rooms with me. You can bring the girls. We have to talk."

Brett shouted across: "Not me, Duke! Not me!"

"Well, bring the damn girls, anyway!"

A little wind soughed down the street. Most of the lights had gone out. Windows were shuttered. The place was like a ghost town. The word had gone around. A man who had tried to follow the Shylao into their secret precincts and steal the secret of The Virility Gene had returned.

When they were ensconced in Selkas's rooms in the best hotel in town, the dynaman said: "We can start from that assumption. Carshder must have found them."

"They found him," said Brett, and he giggled, and stopped giggling, and looked at the girls, draped half-naked on the bed, and Selkas ignored the welpac and went on speaking in his heavy voice.

"The starting line is at the interface between the Shylao and their agents. The actual place of transference changes continually. Bribes can have an effect."

"So you bribed an enforcer to—"

"He was a supplies shuttle pilot, in fact."

"Was?"

"The Shylao don't seem to mind, one way and another; but I did."

Hook looked at the dynaman reflectively. Selkas had a band of glitter synthisilk wrapped around his left tentacle, just where a wrist credit card would be implanted. He'd bought information and shut the mouth of his informant. He'd sent Carshder—or Carshder had been working in partnership, it hardly mattered now—and the Krifman was horribly dead. If the Shylao didn't really mind that one of their employees had betrayed them, they had awful methods of keeping their secrets. Again Hook gained the sense of wheels working within wheels. Probably, he decided, this dynaman Selkas was working for his econorg with a view to moving in.

Multi-system conglomerates like to back sure things. They wouldn't want to do the hard work. But the day was inevitably approaching when nothing would keep them away. Hook knew he was only marginally concerned over the econorgs. There were others in the whirlpool of stars,

84

others whom he knew well, who would sniff this racket and space in. Then there would be real trouble.

Selkas had taken a kill-'em pill and was now perfectly sober.

He laid out his proposition.

It boiled down to simplicity—and that, of course, pleased Ryder Hook, a firm believer in simplicity in skullduggery—and it totalled up to madness and potential death in the same ghastly way that Carshder had died. Selkas would obtain the information on the interface and Hook would go in.

"You can do it, Duke," said Selkas. "In the short time we've met I've formed an opinion on you."

"Yeah," said Brett, sitting cuddling one of the girls who had come around, taken a kill-'em pill, and was seeking to interest a fresh customer in her wares. "Yeah. He's good, is Duke Everest. But these Shylao have all the aces."

Hook knew that Selkas would expect him to talk payment. Of course, Hook would always talk money. It remained a fascinating subject and a firm favorite. Equally of course he had no intention whatsoever of going and sticking his head into whatever mess had destroyed Carshder. Selkas had no lever to make him move.

To cover his thoughts and to gain time, Hook said: "I need a drink. Do you have any decent stuff, Selkas?"

Selkas dialed out and a serving robot trundled in. This was the best hotel in town—Hook wasn't sure what the place was called apart from Wearyville—and Hook helped himself. Then, about to speak his mind to Selkas, he heard the incoming signal alarm in the cocoon. The dynaman grunted some quick apology, and went into a long supposedly private conversation over his private communications set. Hook could hear what he was saying; but the distant caller was inaudible.

". . . only a temporary set back, controller. I am setting up another operation. A sap—yes—Duke Everest. You might check on him. You never know. Yes, controller, I understand the urgency..." A pause. Then: "If Interstell-Imp are moving, and Mos-Kraishoi, I agree there is urgency." A pause. "Are there any other econorgs I might expect to encounter?" Pause. "I see. Well, this sap Everest will do the job. I'm convinced of that. Yes, yes, controller, I understand. Yes. I know we do not want to move prematurely, but... I see..." Pause. "If Everest fails, and we cannot be certain he will succeed, we will have to bring in a full exploratory team."

Hook noted the dynaman's discomfiture.

"I agree, controller, this will alarm the other econorgs. But so far our people have failed. Oh, yes, you had best, controller, report the loss of Taynor Carshder to his family. Yes, a great pity, a great loss to the econorg, a fine man. Yes. Well, if Everest cannot do it, then we will bring in a full planetary exploration team. We will just have to be quicker than the other econorgs."

A long pause ensued then, and Hook read on the dynaman's Krifman face all the signs of apoplectic fury, of controlled resentment, and of the awakening of personal caution. Finally: "I will give the sap Everest three days Krif. After that space in a full team. If we have to fight Interstell-Imp it won't be the first time."

Selkas cut the connection. Hook realized the dynaman must hold a pretty high exec position in his econorg to be able to speak to a controller like that. Probably they were on a level of authority. Multi-system conglomerates liked to work it like that, put two efficient and ruthless men against each other for the promotion each deserved and only one would achieve. Hook went on drinking, making each drink spin out and watching Brett as he pulled the girl's clothes off. She was nice if a little scrawny.

Brett chuckled. "I need some Virility Gene right now."

"Go into the next room, Brett!" commanded the dynaman.

The welpac chuckled again, pawing the girl, who laughed shrilly. "Sure, Selkas, you humming hunk of electricity! Can't you manage it yet, then?"

Hook knew dynamen could lead a full sexual life. Probably Selkas could do more things than Brett dreamed of. Certainly, Brett was back in the room again quickly enough, flushed of face still, his tail drooping, looking for a drink and a chew of stim-gum. The girl followed, patting her hair, looking bored.

Selkas the dynaman laughed crudely.

"You sure need The Virility Gene, Brett! That the best you can do? Haw!"

Brett said nothing but found his drink and stim-gum.

Here, saw Hook, was an example of the terrible power possession of The Virility Gene would confer. The Virility Gene, in tablet form or by injection, both increased the pleasure of the act and prolonged it. Some fantastic records had been set. Men and women would go to extreme lengths to gain possession of The Virility Gene. Any single econorg who controlled its sale would become immeasurably more powerful than it had been before. And—if the Boosted Men gained absolute control? Then, Hook told himself, with a decision he did not relish at all, he'd have to try to do something positive instead of this pleasant baiting of the econorg-dynaman while he waited for Shaeel and Karg.

"What's your econorg, Selkas?"

The dynaman's eyes flashed to his tentacle wrist. The glitter scarf still wrapped safely there.

"Yeah," said Brett, trying to get back. "You're an organization man if ever I smelled one. You ain't a loner."

"As you are working for me, there is no harm. ZZI."

"ZZI," said Brett. "A big one."

Hook knew that ZZI was a Krifman-based econorg. All multi-system conglomerates were composed of many different races and were spread out over many different solar systems; from this they gained their strength. Any individu-

87

al's allegiance must be given first to his econorg. Only after that were considerations of race, of creed, of color, of anything else, allowed any expression at all. The econorg must come first.

But of course these massive groupings of economic power had had to have beginnings. RCI had begun on Earth. ZZI was originally Krifman. Nuke-Chem had started with the mals.

"You know ZZI is very powerful." Selkas clearly was not sure just how far to go. "You people without credit cards may feel at home down here on Shyle; but that won't last long."

Was the dynaman trying to warn them, help them, even?

Brett jumped in. "Who said I ain't got a credit card?"

"And he went to university, too," said Hook.

"My choice of words, my semantic continuity, my occasional lapses into the demotic, my dear Duke, are entirely deliberate and a response to the provocative challenge of clunkheads like you."

"You might take Brett on in ZZI," said Hook. "He fancies a change."

"You get me the secret of Vilgene and it's a deal."

"Hear that, Brett? You get the man that killed Carshder and he'll open the pearly gates to ZZI."

"You're a right chancroid bastard, Ho—Duke!"

"Just remember your choppers!"

Selkas did not like the trend of the conversation. He darted a look at Hook that the evil character read as being an admission of uncertainty. Let the cocooned idiot sweat!

"I'll expect you to be ready, Duke, as soon as I have the interface."

It would not be clever to let rip with a downright no at this stage. "I'll see you around," said Hook. Then, with an insolence he felt remarkably well justified given the circumstances, he said: "You'd better pay Brett for his assistance. A little money-metal now would work wonders."

Brett perked up as the dynaman counted out money-metal.

"Like being back in the stone age," fumed Selkas, counting cash, his wrist credit card hidden under the scarf.

"You'll get used to it, dynaman."

"When the econorgs get here—"

"Ah, but," said Ryder Hook. "Make that if."

Hook and Brett left Selkas to his girls and went outside into the darkness and started off for their flier. Hook heard the footfall in plenty of time to unlimber the Martin Mega and to step back into a doorway. His left hand caught Brett's elbow. "Stand in here, and keep still."

"Wha—?"

"*Still!*"

A breathy voice sounded from the darkness. Hook could have used a pair of uv glasses right then, even a pair of ir's would have done. The voice sounded petulant.

"Where'd he go, Taynor Line?"

"He came out of that gonil Selkas's room. I know that—"

"And I know that, too!" The voices drifted away. "When you do find him, Line, I want him dead! Capish? Dead!"

9

Ryder Hook had no wish to become embroiled with idiots who wanted to see him dead. Many people had wanted to see him dead; but he was still around. He neither knew nor cared what had happened to them.

The two voices out there whispered fiercely as their owners squabbled.

"Oxymoron, Line! He's only an eczema-sniffing spirochaete sap! You should be able to rubberize him before your first tutorial!"

"It's all right for you, Taynor Synker! You don't have the trouble I have with the rubberization process."

"Why do I have to be burdened with a septic pustule like you for a partner."

"Why, you leprous carcinoma sucker, Synker—I'm every bit as good as you!"

"You remind me of that inefficient teleplay we say back on Lardhock. That three-foot hunchbacked Sirian killer-fwoq—"

"Killer what?"

"You heard me. You pronounce it, then!"

The voices drifted away. Ryder Hooked wanted to laugh.

He'd met this sorry pair before. Line and Synker. The biggest goofs in the whirlpool of stars—only they, with a wit derived from rubberization of the brain faculties, called the galaxy the cesspool of stars. That was because they were always in it. Up to the eyeballs. Brett should have no trouble with them.

"Who were those two incredible clunkheads, Hook?"

"Synker and Line. Two undercover agents. They work for whoever pays 'em, and they're always on the bread line."

"No wonder." Brett chuckled—he, like most men who could chuckle at the right time, found humor in ludicrous situations and ludicrous people. It took all kinds to make up a galaxy. "I've a mind to walk up and ask 'em who's hiring them to kill us."

"They'd probably tell you. They are amateurs."

"Still and all, Hook, someone else is out to—"

"They always are."

"When do you think Selkas will have the information on the interface?"

"Who knows? I'm not going, that's for sure."

"Not going! But—"

"I don't believe in getting myself killed, Brett."

"No, but—"

"Look, don't worry about that sorry pair, Line and Synker. They will have goofed-up on their last contract and have conned some fresh idiot into staking them. They're always bumming around. They probably can't afford a decent energy weapon. They'll try to be big-time chopper-men with a Zag or some even more ancient projectile pistol. Mind you—" here Hook recalled some of the stunts Jack Kinch had pulled. "Mind you, a solid bullet can smear you."

"Have they ever completed a successful mission?"

"I tend to doubt it."

"I wonder if they've ever seen a man shot—guts and blood spraying out—?"

"From the way they talk I think they cannot have."

"Perhaps I'll give 'em a demonstration—if they bother me, Duke."

"Your privilege, Brett, your privilege."

"They sounded like Homo sapiens."

"Oh, they are, Brett, they are. Both of 'em. Saps."

All sounds of the two amateur undercover agents having died, Hook and Brett walked peacefully on.

"Mind you," said Hook, reflectively. "You can't be too hard on 'em. I mean—they do the best they can. I bear 'em no grudges—"

That made Brett laugh.

Then he sobered. "It still does not explain why you talked to Selkas like that, and now say you're not going along with his plans." By this time Brett recognized that his own hold over Hook—a hold that had existed only in his own mind—had become so tenuous as to be invisible.

No doubt there were at this very minute sordid little scenes like the one between the dynaman and Hook going on all over the planet of Shyle. The planet could be a pleasant place. There existed scenery of the greatest grandeur. The forests extended, wild and so far untamed. The prairies would support herds of livestock. The seas rolled into white beaches clean and unpolluted. Somewhere on this planet a secret was to be discovered, and econorgs would move in, and if they would genuflect to planned ecology and planetary conservation, their powers were such that if it suited their books not to take cognizance of human dignity in a natural environment, then they would disregard it entirely.

And the Boosted Men would finish anything the econorgs started. There was much good in multi-system conglomerates and Ryder Hook recognized that. He was looking for good in the Novamen and so far had found none.

So what was taking place in those sordid little scenes of intrigue would affect far more than this single planet.

Abruptly, Hook halted.

Brett started to say: "Wha—?" an expression to which he was becoming addicted.

Hook pushed the welpac into another of the shadowed doorways lining the street. The darkness breathed about them.

"A spick-probe, picking us up," he said. His skull-mounted antihomotropic devices could pick out a spick-probe. He lied quickly to Brett. "I've a resonator in my pocket."

"If they shoot—"

Hook was already working on the door. "In here."

They tumbled through into a store, the dusty space piled with boxes and bales, starlight streaking with faint smears through high windows. "Watch out for buckets and brooms. The cleaning robots hereabouts aren't all that careful."

From the crack of the door Hook peered down the street. He really must invest in a pair of uv or ir glasses. He could see nothing in the hazy starlight and the moon hung so low it merely emphasized the shadows.

Brett was already running through to the back. Hook closed the door gently, tumbled the lock he had picked, and ran after the welpac. A spick-probe could, depending on the amount of credit expended on the model, penetrate clapboarding and plastic sheeting. It could be stopped by steel. The stores in this section had been run up out of plastic sheeting.

"Come on, Hook! We've gotta run for it!"

Hook started to run. Then he stopped. What the hell!

He was being chased about like a greenhorn straight out of Space Academy, with only a university degree to show to the galaxy. He bore the wielder of the spick-probe no ill will and he felt he would like to make the fellow understand that. Just that Hook sometimes got tired of running. He'd always run from trouble if he could, of course; but, sometimes...

He followed Brett after all, running out to the starshot

night at the back of the stores. Here service trucks stood silent. A robot slumbered in his packing-crate shelter.

He was an old robot, a massive construct of metalloy arms and legs, a dumpy cranium, staring lenses. He was a perfectly good specimen of the species of robot designed in the old days for manual labor. Hook woke him up. He simply bellowed in one ear—a mike pick-up situated where an ear should be on a sap—"Roust, tinman! Roust!"

"I am at your service, sir."

"There are thieves breaking into the stores. They've bypassed the alarm circuits on the door. I hope you will be able to deal with them."

"I can deal with thieves, sir."

"Remember your programming, tinman."

"I am unable, sir, to forget my programming. It circuits on a closed-tape-loop through my what you would call head, sir. As you know, sir. I will treat them with the respect flesh and blood should be accorded, even if it be thieving flesh and blood."

"Someone fed him a dictionary," said Brett.

"He's a nice old robot, though. Go on, tinman. Do your duty."

"Very good, sir."

The robot whirred and clicked a few times. He was pretty old. Hook guessed no robot like that had been offered for sale as new for a thousand years, terrestrial. The tinman toddled off and Hook and Brett sprinted through the night toward the end of the street. Brett wanted to head for their flier.

"No, Brett. Wait until we know it's clear."

A sudden succession of bangs erupted at the rear of the store. It was too damn difficult to see in the tricky light. But Hook could swear the robot came barreling out backward, smoking, spraying parts, his head flying off and spinning. But it was too dark to see properly...

The whine of an out-of-phase motor screeched down from the sky. A brilliant white circle of illumination bathed the whole area at the back of the store. Hook blinked. A metallic voice from the flier crackled. "This is the police! Stand still!"

Hook took a single look. The robot was trundling around in circles that spiraled inwards smaller and smaller. His head *had* gone spinning off. He *was* gushing smoke. His parts *were* spraying off—linkages, transistors, circuits, locrasms, metalloy casings—all just as Hook had fancied he had glimpsed before.

Two dark figures burst from the back of the store. They wore all-black coveralls, with black hoods. One of them carried a spick-probe; Hook could see the black box and the detector aerial quite clearly. The other lifted his gun and fired and with a crack the searchlight went out.

A wash of radiance gushed from the flier. A leach field.

Hook saw the two men desperately attempting to flee back into the building. They moved in slow-time, slower and slower. Eventually they merely moved their legs feebly and did not stir. The flier let down and enforcers jumped out.

"Time to go, Brett."

"Yes," Brett shivered. "The Shylao are late on the ball; but when they arrive, they come!"

"That leach field really slowed those two gonils down."

"Let's get to the flier and leave, Hook! I'm not so sure I want to find The Virility Gene, after all!"

"Ah, but," said Ryder Hook. "It makes the old blood tingle though!"

He opened his eyes and saw the metalloy interior of the flier. The alarm was ringing from the communications console. Hook rolled over and snapped off the irritating noise. "Yes?"
"Duke Everest?"

"Who wants him?"

"Jon Selkas."

"Wait."

Hook felt fine. He did not have a headache, the air smelled sweet and fresh in the flier, he was healthily hungry and looked forward to breakfast. He swung his legs to the deck and without disturbing Brett who slumbered away on the other bunk, bent to the microphone.

"Everest."

"It's today. Meet me in my rooms midday."

The communications rig went dead.

Ryder Hook stood up and stretched, and scratched his back, ran his fingers through his thick brown hair, yawned. He washed thoroughly and set the tea to brewing. Then he set about preparing the reconstituted bacon and eggs and egg pudding for Brett. It was going to be an interesting day.

The old proverb that you seldom eavesdropped on any good opinions of yourself was probably quite true, and Ryder Hook, who usually tried to listen to what was going on inside a room before he entered, valued that for the information it gave to the true feelings of people who were all smarmy to your face.

Outside Selkas' room he paused, for only a moment in intention, to make sure, and he heard Selkas almost shouting on the communications rig he had inside his cocoon.

"You sure! Now look, controller, that makes it six. Six! I can handle two econorgs easily enough, I've done it, you know that. But I figure six is pulling too many gees."

Hook waited. He could not hear what the controller was saying; but he waited for Selkas to speak again. It wasn't polite, was it, to barge in when a guy was on the phone?

"All right, controller. I'll expect a team, then. This Duke Everest can still go in—what? Nothing? You sure you've no dossier on a Duke Everest?" A pause. "That's very strange.

He strikes me as the kind of man who can take care of himself, a natural troubleshooter—or troublemaker, more like. He handles himself with assurance, not like the usual loner. You'd better keep looking. Probably Everest is an alias. Check." A pause. Then: "I see. Well, RCI are a fagged-out conglomerate, anyway, controller. I don't anticipate trouble from them. It's Interstell-Imp and GCC we've to watch out for. Check. Bye."

Hook knocked and walked in.

Jon Selkas looked just the same, squatting there in his womb surrogate, the golden gleams of sunlight glancing from the cocoon's metalloy hull and transparent canopy. He lifted a cup and Hook smelled the coffee and made a face.

"Coffee, Duke?"

"No, thanks."

If he added that he considered coffee a barbarian's drink, and that tea was a civilized drink, that peice of information would go into the dossier ZZI had on Duke Everest. Eventually a computer would cross match it with the dossier on Ryder Hook. He knew that would happen; he just wanted to prolong the agony. Like The Virility Gene.

"You can take your own flier. The interface is across planet on the eastern continent. They're shipping out a hundred tonnes."

"Can't use the flier. That's Brett's."

"This is a new story! You mean I'm to supply transport?"

"Shouldn't be too difficult with the muscle ZZI pull."

"I'll attend to it."

"Another thing. D'you know a couple of operatives called Line and Synker?"

"Those clowns!"

"Some one's been misguided enough to hire 'em to kill me."

Selkas made a note. "I'll see to it." He did not look pleased. "How did you let them get on to you?"

"I didn't. They had your rooms cased. There were two other guys, choppermen by the look of 'em. The local Shyle goons picked them up last night."

"I know about them. Interstell-Imp."

Jon Selkas was distinctly upset.

"Sure," said Ryder Hook. "It means your operation's blown. All the econorgs are breathing down your neck. One thing. Don't be too hard on Line and Synker. They're clowns, but they mean well."

"It could be, Everest, you attracted them here."

"Not a chance. Why should high-power muscle men bother with a prospector like me? Or Brett? They had your rooms staked out." He shook his head. "You power men of the conglomerates c'n fight all you like. Just leave me out."

That was true.

"I wonder about you, Duke. Really wonder."

"Just let me know the interface, show me the transport and point me in the right direction. Hunting treasure is one thing—tangling with econorgs is another game entirely."

He was making his point. Hook's persuasive powers could often—not always—be relied on to pull the wool over an organization man's eyes. They tended to think in straight lines.

The moment Jon Selkas had mentioned RCI Hook knew he was committed. Hook hooked. RCI besides being the econorg that had trained up Ryder Hook and, through their use of him as a guinea pig in the Powerman Project, given him these quasipowers he possessed, were also the same econorg that had created fully Boosted Man, and had been taken over by them, and was a mere tool in the hands of the Novamen. Smell a Boosted Man, said Hook, and you smelled corruption and death.

He should know.

He was half a Boosted Man himself.

He roused himself, glared at Selkas, took the directions

98

and barged off. If the dynaman wondered what had got into his new recruit for the suicide Shylao Stakes, he'd never guess the truth.

If only, considered Ryder Hook, alias Duke Everest, if only he could one day find some redeeming feature in a Boosted Man! When that day came, if it ever did, he would wonder what to do. If he was really as rough and tough as he was made out to be, there would never be room in his head for these thoughts—especially with all that organic circuitry stuffed there by EAS!

"You'd better go out the back way, Duke," Selkas had said, and so Hook barged out and over a couple of roofs and so down the back alley among the junk and the crates and the robots. He would have liked to have gone back to the store and asked out there how the tinman was getting on. When robots got that old they were very often not considered candidates for rebuilding. Hook was not becoming gushy over an impersonal robot; just that to Hook even artificial life held a wonder that could not be taken too lightly. Every time he was forced to kill he knew a portion of himself died along with the victim. Even a Boosted Man—a thing of immaterial spirit and a parody of flesh and blood—contained the magical seeds of life. Many men deserved to die for the deeds they had committed; but Hook would not be the first to press the trigger. If he was a subtly complex man of the galaxy that was a mere matter of conditioning. The strangeness would have been grotesque had he been a mere black and white figure of remorseless destruction, so beloved of the illiterate TY channels.

Mind you, he'd punch any curd in the eye who tried to patronize him...

If the curd saw by eyesight, of course...

He took himself off to the rendezvous point arranged by Selkas down by the sewage-plant recycling stores. A few robots trundled about their tasks. Hook wrinkled up his nose at the smell seeping from the plant. Nothing was one hundred percent in this galaxy. And there was the galaxy, that whirlpool of stars, and all of space to roam in, away up there, and here he was stuck down on this ball of mud.

Well—all the galaxy was, really, to breathing human beings was a collection of balls of mud.

The balls of mud were the important constituents.

A flier slanted in and Hook saw without expression that Selkas had had the forethought to pick one without obvious ZZI markings. The pilot stepped out. She was a girl, a sap, very nice, very sweet. She wore a helmet; but Hook knew she was very nice, very sweet, by the way she walked, the way her spun-synthsilk trousers clung to her thighs, the way her tunic was loosely unzipped at her throat. She came toward him, swaying, unstrapping her helmet and loosening it. Her hair dyed a fashionable corn gold, fluffed. She smiled with that sweet smile that so disarmed.

Her dinky little dis-gel gun was in her hand and pointing at Ryder Hook and he remained perfectly still.

"So you were in with Carshder, Taynor Klark."

"No, Tayniss Sharon. Anyway, haven't you heard about Carshder?"

"Oh, yes. I must admit I didn't know whether to laugh or cry."

"Either will ruin your makeup."

He wasn't going to get to her this way. This Sharon was sharp. She'd already had him dumped into space once. Brett the welpac had said that Sharon did not like doing her killing herself. So:

"Where's Rhus?"

"He's around."

In the flier, probably, aiming his damned great stun gun.

"You're working for ZZI, Klark. Or should it be Everest?"

"Take your pick."

"In that case I'll call you Duke. It fits. Now, get in the flier.

100

We're going to do exactly as that gonil Selkas has laid it out for you to do. Check?"

"You're buying yourself an awful lot of trouble—"

"Into the flier!" She jerked the gun threateningly.

"Did you hire Line and Synker to—"

"Those two half wits? You must be joking."

As they walked toward the flier, Hook said: "Tell me, Tayniss Sharon. How did Carshder and Michael Michael explain away the scene in the cabin?"

"Stop talking and get in. Rhus will settle you if you do not do exactly as I say. I'm in charge now, Duke."

10

Ryder Hook particularly wanted to know about Michael Michael.

The Doorn, Win Fareng, had employed those Riffian enforcers working with Michael Michael, and for the Doorn Ryder Hook had—among a varied assortment of emotions—the liveliest respect. The bastards might be mindlessly motivated mechanics; they were damned clever. If a Doorn considered Michael Michael a useful tool to employ, then Hook wanted to know what had happened.

He repeated his question as the flier leaped for the sky. Rhus at the controls kept a tight scrutiny of all the tell-tales. As far as Hook could make out, automatically checking the board, they were not spotted.

"Michael Michael?" said Sharon. "Forget him. He's out of it. There was some fuss in *Vandeneuf*; but whatever it was, Stellroutes didn't want the scandal. Rhus here threw Michael Michael off the scent three planets back."

"Good for you, Rhus."

"Were I not acting under orders of Tayniss Sharon, Klark, I would smash your face in."

"You can do that later, Rhus," said Sharon, impatiently. "And we're calling this curd Duke Everest now."

"There's nothing in a change of name for a loner."

"That's right," said Hook. "Let's see—what econorg are you with?"

Sharon turned away, busying herself with the maps. She looked up. "Get us on course, chancroid, and no slip ups."

Hook fancied for some reason, she was losing her calmness.

The flier turned accurately on to course and Hook had merely to check the autopilot kept them targeted for their destination in the eastern continent. The flier flew high. There was nothing to see outside save the streaming lines and glinting spiracles as the clouds speared far below, the blue-blackness above, with three fat stars showing a ghostly image. The flier began to slant down. She was a Mollins Puma, a useful model, if not up to standards of refinement found on more expensive models like the Tiger, and she brought them down and out exactly on the button.

Rhus took her off auto and handled her well on manuals. Most Krifmans were good with machines. Hook looked overside.

He had often wondered just how far along whatever freakish evolutionary road the Boosted Men were following his own conditioning had taken him. He felt morally certain he was different in many areas from a Boosted Man who had gone through the full treatment. He fancied he had had experiments performed on him that had proved unacceptable to the scientists of RCI and had been abandoned, not to be carried out on the men who had been turned into Boosted Men. That being so, Hook often fancied he carried within his amazing body—amazing because it was amazing—capacities of which the Novamen could know nothing.

Below them the ground showed a pleasant plain, dotted with trees, with the running forms of sextupeds, with well-defined trails where game animals trotted down to the water. Beneath one clump of trees toward which they were settling there was glint of sunlight on a weapon, no suspicious movement—but to Hook's heightened senses, there *was* something...

He threw himself across the cabin, barged Rhus off the controls, bashed them with vicious efficiency, sent the flier screaming downward at enormous acceleration.

"You idiot!" screamed Sharon before the forces threw her down. Rhus was trying to claw back and falling. Hook felt those gee forces tugging at him like cobwebs in a nighted graveyard. He let the flier scream downward. The blast from the trees belched luridly above them, drenching the cabin in actinic light. They all blinked, seeing novae exploding in their retinas. Hook waited... He waited until the last minute, until two more titanic blasts shook the air beyond them, then he flattened the flier out. Sharon could not scream.

She blacked out. Rhus heaved up, and collapsed. Hook merely let his knees flex a little more. His blood channeled around his body in ways designed by those surgeon-medical-bioscientists building men for hard labor on heavy-gravity worlds.

Hook took the flier in to a fast landing beneath a further clump of trees. He fancied they would have little time in getting clear. From the medkit he took a hypo and not without interest pulled Sharon's trousers down and rolled her on her stomach. Her cheeks were beautifully rounded and firm. He placed the spray against her skin, golden and glowing, and pressed the stud. By the time he had done the same for Rhus, Sharon's eyelids fluttered. By the time Rhus came around, Hook was hurling gear to the grass. He half-turned and bellowed.

"Get your kit out here, you clunkheads! The flier'll be over in a minute to fry us! *Move!*"

They needed no further encouragement.

Soon a mound of kit lumped on the grass. Rhus

shouldered a massive heap, including a Krifman long-barrel model twenty two. Sharon picked up cooking gear and food. Hook stripped a length of wiring from the cabin lighting, frayed it out, started tying the ends to the controls.

"Hurry it up, Duke!"

"I'm coming now." He jumped out, left the cabin door open. He jerked the wiring. The flier took off as though under human guidance and then, with a final jerk, Hook cut in the autos. The flier flew steadily toward the horizon.

"Let's get going!" said Rhus. He glanced at Sharon.

Hook went to the edge of the trees. The ground lay like an undulating sea of grass, a savannah that would be pleasurable if they were not being hunted like wild animals. Now was the time for a decision. He said: "Stay,"

Sharon said: "They'll backtrack the flier's course to here."

"I know. We'll run when they—ah! *There!*"

The Mollins Puma erupted in a central core of fire and a jaggedly expanding blot of black smoke. Wreckage plummeted groundward. The shock waves blattered among the trees.

"Run!" yelled Hook.

He started running. He wouldn't damn well stop for the other two. He'd get his tail in among the trees of the next clump and hunker down. Then, perhaps, he'd look to see how Sharon and Rhus were getting along.

They made it. Sharon flopped down, panting, her face glowing with crimson beneath the golden tan. Rhus, too, panted from the effort. Hook decided he'd better pant, too, and drew a few artistic whoops of air.

"You run damn fast, Duke!"

"I find the promise of a tickler up my spine has that effect."

They looked out.

A flier skimmed toward the clump of trees they had just left. It was an armored job, very lethal, with guns sticking out all over, or so it seemed to the heightened imagination. It circled twice and then flew off.

"If they'd checked us with homotropes," said Rhus.

"They didn't," said Sharon. She eased the straps of her pack. The straps made the thin synthidenim of her tunic strain against her breasts. Hook looked away. He had more important things to do than admire a pretty girl's breasts—but then, how could there be more important things than doing just that in the entire galaxy? Unless what followed was more important, and that brought up The Virility Gene...

He knew that if the flier had checked, his own antihomotrop gear would have dazzled the instruments. But it was nice not to have to think of another explanation involving Filker Fredericks.

Ryder Hook could have thought of better companions to have along on this infuriating adventure; but Tayniss Sharon seemed still to imagine she was running the show. Hook's Martian Mega snugged at Rhus's waist, big and lethal. Rhus had emptied the dis-gel magazine. It must seem to Sharon she ran the show.

"If we go on now they'll see us and pick us up," said Sharon.

"Yes." Hook didn't wait for Rhus to speak. "That's one way of getting in."

"You don't mind? After Carshder?"

"You have any better ideas?"

She did not answer directly. "Let's eat."

Hook said: "I just hope your back-up team is up to the job, Sharon. We're up against the big boys now."

"How d'you know we've a back-up team?" demanded Rhus.

Hook didn't bother to reply. Sharon said: "Act your age, Rhus! This chancroid Duke is something special. I thought so from the first."

Again Hook didn't say anything.

They broke open the rations and ate sparingly. Maybe these two might be useful, at that, wondered Hook, chewing.

The time was not yet ripe for him to ask for his weapons back. If he had them they would merely give Rhus an extra itchy finger and a good excuse.

A most charming and lovely young lady had once called Ryder Hook a star-spanning man of the future. What he appreciated most about that description was the word 'future.' Hook believed in having a future. He did not believe in doing things conducive to abrupt endings to his future.

"We go on," said Sharon when they had eaten. "We go steadily. You know the way, Duke. Lead on."

"MacDuke will do just that, tayniss."

Even a Krifman would understand the allusion to a scribe dead these eighty-five centuries.

As they plodded on Hook came to the tentative conclusion that judging by what had happened to Carshder, who must have done something foolish similar to their actions now, they would not be shot out of hand by the Shyloa. Enforcers had been having a go at the Mollins Puma. So that meant that Carshder had gone farther than they had so far reached. He might have been doing his stuff at a different interface, probably almost certainly had been: Hook kept on.

That old F-type Jarhed shone down. Insect cream kept the nuisances away. The sun declined. A breeze got up. They saw extremely large herds of six-legged game animals, and Hook wondered how the delightful ts Sharon would face up to a rich and juicy steak. He'd try her this night, as ever was.

When they made camp, with a fire shielded from observation by a leaf-woven windbreak, and they ate the juicy steaks from the animal Rhus had shot, Hook notched up another coup for Sharon. She tucked into the rich natural food like a trooper. Compatible bacteria must exist on this planet for men to live here at all. The food was rich and good—and safe.

Early on the following morning they saw three fliers in train go winging over a range of distant hills, purple and green in the slanting sunlight. Later they saw another lone flier skimming low between rounded hills.

"Trying to slip under the radar—" said Rhus.

Even as he spoke the flier exploded. A bright flash of flame and a greasy ball of black smoke were all that remained.

"He didn't fly low enough," said Hook, and trudged on.

Certain unmistakable signs were beginning to add up and to pose a worry to Hook. The reaction of the Shyloan enforcers in guarding the interface indicated that the Syhloa were growing tired of interference. They sold their Virility Gene at enormous prices to selected agencies. They guarded the point of transaction. Econorgs had not yet come on to the scene. But everyone knew the econorgs were coming in very soon, and here he was, Ryder Hook, as an example of that, supposedly working for ZZI. GCC and Interstell-Imp were also involved. Six, the dynaman Selkas had said. There was RCI... Finding out about The Boosted Men's RCI conglomerate was the only thing bringing Hook here now.

So maybe the Shyloa wouldn't bother to capture them and thus give Hook a chance to blow 'em all up from inside, which was the formula. He'd do it the hard way, if needs be. Sharon and Rhus, of course, were mere pawns, acting on their behalf and thus mere grains to be crushed between millstones.

The thought did occur to Ryder Hook, alias Duke Everest, that he, too, was a loner acting on his own behalf; but the thought had no power to impress him. He'd lived with it for too long. He didn't want to be any other than a loner.

The second night Rhus and Sharon made love and Hook heard them thumping and thrashing away in the grass. He ignored it for about two minutes flat and then he bellowed: "Can't you two let a man get some sleep? You're not using Virility Gene so don't try to impress me with your performance. You're like a couple of hippopotami run out of mud."

They went very quiet. Then Rhus whispered something, and Sharon giggled, and Hook knew they were telling each other he was jealous. He was, too—but not of Sharon and Rhus.

So he was getting to be old. So all right. On the morrow he'd give Sharon something she wouldn't forget if she wiggled her bottom at him again. He was as grouchy and soreheaded as he had been in a long time when they set off in the morning.

Mid morning brought another string of patrol fliers. They curved overhead and the trio hid in a clump of trees. When the fliers had gone Rhus laughed and said: "They flew right over us and did not pick us up. They couldn't have paid much credit for their surveillance equipment."

Hook didn't disabuse him.

Yet again, that afternoon, when they spotted a watch tower rising beyond a hill as they wended over the lower slopes, Hook's homotrop dazzlement equipment buried in his skull enabled them to creep up undetected. Rhus shot the two guards. They had had two arms; but that was all anyone could say of them after the Krifman long-barrel model twenty two got through.

Hook climbed up the tower, a plastic prefabricated construct, and checked the equipment. It was high quality. He smashed it with his boots. Sharon panted up after him, looking mean.

"What did you do that for, you stupid animal!"

"Animals have tender feelings too, you know, Sharon."

He swiveled the high-power tele-binoculars which he had left undamaged. "Look over there."

He directed her observation onward past the continuing flank of the hill and down into the valley. Spread out were huts, filling stations, flier parks, and, at the far end, a prefabricated hotel that would not have looked out of place beside some econorg-executive's private beach on a pleasure planet.

Sharon sighed a deep and satisfying breath.

"That's it!"

Through the observation screen they saw the traffic. Tankers coming in, dropping down on to the park. Pipes leading through to calibrating stations, distribution pumping centers, and on to the filling stations. Here waited a line of tankers marked with various symbols, one or two of which Hook recognized.

"The econorgs will go green when they see this!" Sharon was deeply excited. She was also aroused, which surprised Hook. Her nipples thrust hard against the synthidenim. Maybe it was the thought of all that Virility Gene over there.

"A milli liter costs a fortune! And there are tons of it there!"

"Just let me get my hands on a tankful!" breathed Rhus.

"I always thought you were a small-time piker," said Hook. He didn't much care for Rhus. The Krifman felt so sure of himself and yet had already exhibited incompetence it hurt.

Rhus swung savagely at Hook. Hook blocked the blow. Sharon yelled; but Hook fancied this was a good a time as any, and kicked the Krifman. He kicked hard. He followed the kick by ducking the instinctive return blow and sticking his thumb into the Krifman's right eye. Rhus yelled. Rhus would always yell when the going got tough—an aphorism, a useful aphorism.

110

Hook went on moving and then Sharon yelled: "Put him down, Duke! You drop him and I'll shoot! Bring him back in here!"

Hook turned his head. Sharon had a Delling centered on his back.

"You use that on me, Sharon, and either I'll drop Rhus over the side and he'll break his goddamn neck, or he'll get melted along with me."

"Just put him down inside the tower, unhurt."

"Oh, he's hurt all right." But Hook brought Rhus back inside, and stood him up, and brushed his clothes down. "His pride's hurt." Rhus hadn't known what hit him. He stood, eyes unfocused, the right one smarting like hell, shaking, bewildered.

"He'll get over it, Sharon. Then the goml will try to kill me and I'll have to settle with him. What then?"

"When we get The Virility Gene, you two can slug it out."

"A real lady, you are, and no mistake."

Then Sharon noticed what had happened to the Martian Mega during the little fight. It was in Hook's belt. He saw her reaction.

"Sure, Sharon. When you were yapping at me with your dinky little dis-gel I could have blasted you."

"But—you didn't, Duke. You didn't."

"Remember, Sharon. I stuck a revivifying spray on your bottom. Maybe that hypnotised me."

"You chancroid!"

"Ah, happy memories."

Rhus breathed raggedly. He would kill as soon as he could; that appeared certain. Hook had only made matters worse.

"Duke—" Sharon's breathing was unsteady. She half-held her right hand out to him, in mute appeal. The Delling had flicked back to its place of concealment on her wrist. "Duke—Rhus likes to kill. He—"

"He does your dirty work. I've heard. I suppose you enticed the poor devil of a ZZI pilot who was bringing the flier over—and Rhus killed him?"

"Yes—But I didn't want him killed! I don't—"

"Save it."

But Hook could not forget the look in Sharon's eyes, the way the synthidenim strained as she struggled to get her breathing under control. Maybe The Virility Gene was leaking over there, a thin gossamer wisp from a punctured tank, and she was loosening up and feeling like it. But then, he'd be feeling the same, wouldn't he? All he felt like in that moment about Tayniss Sharon was to belt her on the backside and yell at her to grow up, rather than take steps to do anything about the sexual passion tormenting her.

Of course, he was a rotten bastard. That wasn't news.

Rhus was trying to speak, gargling, holding his throat where a thumb had driven without much consideration for his larynx. Hook did not ignore the Krifman. The dis-gel gun on Hook's left wrist was empty; but the Mega could be out and shooting in time enough.

Hook prodded Sharon a little more.

"You're after the secret. It's all spread out over there for you. What are you waiting for?"

"I—" She licked her lips, glanced at Rhus, swung back to face Hook. "You'll—come with me?"

Hook leered at her. "No, Tayniss Sharon. This is as far as I go."

"But Duke—! I don't understand."

Hook wasn't going to tell her that this was a mere interface, the point at which the Shylao transferred processed supplies of The Virility Gene to their customers. He wasn't going to tell her the next step was to follow the Shylao back to wherever it was they produced Vilgene. Carshder had got as far as this, despite the trigger-happy enforcers. Hook fancied he had as good a chance as that tough Krifman.

"My job ends here, Sharon. I report back. You've been brought here. It's all on a plate for you. Nothing can stop you from waltzing in and taking what you want."

She remained bewildered. "So it seems. But—I still don't understand. My information was that Dynaman Selkas hired you to uncover the Vilgene supply—"

Hook waved a hand grandly toward the valley and the ordered activity.

"There's the proof, gal, over there. Why wait?"

She shook her head, completely undecided.

Normally Hook was an extraordinarily patient man. Sometimes his patience fizzled like a clipped half-second fuse.

"You said you were in charge, Sharon, you were running the show. What the hell are you waiting for? Get on over there! Take all The Virility Gene you want! Go on!"

Her lips firmed. "You're coming with me, Duke."

"You can't make me. You reach for your gun—and I'll shoot you."

"A clumsy great energy gun like yours can't beat a wrist disgel!"

"Don't bank on it. You care to try?"

"No." She bit her lip. "No."

And then Hook saw a further truth about Tayniss Sharon. He didn't know her other names. She was courageous. No doubt about that. She must be possessed of tremendous reserves of energy, of bravery, of sheer womanly guts, to have come as far as she had. She wasn't afraid to try him and see if her Delling could beat his Mega. No—she wasn't afraid. And a kind of sympathy for her took root in Ryder Hook's cold and tough emotions then. She deserved better than a curd like Rhus.

Had Hook thought that by cutting down Rhus where he stood he would materially help Sharon, he would have done so. But he knew that would be no solution.

"By the Great Salvor," she said, and her voice caught in her throat. "I wish I could trust you, Duke Everest!"

"Put it this way. You trust me as much as I trust you."

"I'll kill the gonil!" Rhus managed to gargle.

Clearly, in his distress, he hadn't realized Hook had repossessed himself on his Martian Mega.

Hook's own plans called for a rapid sheeding of Sharon and Rhus, a quick snatch of a flier, and then the careful shadowing of the Shylao on their way back to their primary area, the place where the Vilgene was produced. Sharon and Rhus could have no place in this plan.

"Goodbye, Sharon."

"Goodbye?"

"Yes. You carry on from here."

"But—but, Duke—" It was all clearly far too much for Tayniss Sharon.

Hook made his way down the ladder. He kept his gaze fixed on Rhus and went down by feel. When he touched the ground he called up: "You'd better make yourself scarce. They'll monitor the watch tower."

She didn't answer; but her synthidenimed leg appeared over the edge and she started down. Rhus followed shakily. Hook ran for the nearest cover, a patch of broken ground in the lee of the hill where wild gorse-like plants grew lushly.

He ran fast. He knew Rhus would be sufficiently recovered now to tug out that Krifarm long-barrel model twenty-two and take a shot—and Hook wanted to be invisible by then, so the Krifman would have no target. Hook dived for a thickly profuse bush.

He was in the air, plunging forward, when all along his organo-metal bones, thrilling through his skull, pulsing in his veins, pumping in his arteries, he felt the shattering forces take him and twist and turn him out of being a normal human and thrust him savagely into the near superhuman state of being a Boosted Man.

He hit the ground and rolled over and he moved in speed time.

He was a Boosted Man! A full, one hundred percent Boosted Man!

He could sense the direction of the real Boosted Man from whom this massive display of power pulsed. Whenever Hook came into proximity with a Boosted Man, like tuned crystals resonating, Hook, too, partook of the phenomenal qualities of the Boosted State. He stared up hungrily. He longed—always—for this state of divine hell. He hungered to be a Boosted Man, and yet he knew that the hunger, the desire, the very structure of himself, could only turn into evil as the Boosted Men had themselves succumbed to the artificial and become Novamen.

He expected to see a flier lowering down. In that bright dazzlement of alien sky he could see only high clouds, and a bird, and the brilliance of Jarhed.

He watched the sky. He felt—oh, he felt the fires of heaven and hell consuming him. His brain operated at a phenomenal speed, his nerve endings jumped to the pulsating passage of billions of messages, he was near divine, not a superman—never that!—but so near that he understood as no other human mortal might the temptations that had lured the Boosted Men and destroyed their humanity and so unleashed a blackness upon the galaxy.

When at last he saw the tanker dropping down to the park, saw it land, saw the Boosted Man emerge, he knew he was looking at a Novaman of incredible powers. The resonance had begun when the Boosted Man had been literally kilometers away! Such power awed Hook. Never before had he experienced a transition from his normal state to the Boosted in so powerful and overwhelming a fashion, nor at such a distance. He would see with the preternaturally sharp vision of the Boosted, see and hear, and operate with speeds far outstripping most computers.

With the Boosted Man came a girl and a man Hook recognized. Michael Michael. So the human agent chosen by Win Fareng, one of the Boosted Men's Doorn, had at last traced him here. But had he? Hook watched. The Boosted Man operated in normal time—which was slow time to a Novaman!—and he laughed and chatted with the guards and enforcers who checked him out. The tanker moved in line. So the Boosted Men had at last decided to move in on Shyle. This was the opening. They were pretending to be normal customers. Once they began, their speed-time powers would uncover the Shylao's secret of The Virility Gene. Then the dark power they wielded in the galaxy would become vastly greater. Everything else slipped away into insignificance before the terror of this new development.

11

Ryder Hook had certain things to do before he could deal with the Boosted Man.

How long would the bastard stay in the area?

Never mind about that right now. That quick flash of intuitive sympathy for Sharon had to be put down. Ryder Hook couldn't go skating around the galaxy feeling sorry for girls; that would never do.

Moving in speed time he passed the tower. Sharon stood at the foot of the ladder, one leg lifted, her body half-turned most charmingly. Five rungs above her Rhus had turned fully around, his heels on the rungs. His big Krifman hand rested on the stock of the long-barrel Krifarm. Hook could see the sinews ridged in his hand. The gonil was in the act of aiming to shoot Hook in the back. Hook trusted he had vanished into the bushes before he'd speeded up into fast time. Even so, suppose he hadn't—all Rhus would have seen as Hook dived for the bush would have been his sudden disappearance. The Krifman's eyes would simply report back that Hook had vanished and the man's brain would reassure him that the sap had got away into the bushes. People saw what they wanted to see.

It would be pleasant to do something diabolical to Rhus right now, say jimmying his weapon so the thing blew up when he pressed the trigger. But Rhus offered some protection to Sharon, and the girl had a long way to go before she was safely out of this one. And she was the female chancroid who'd had him dumped into space!

Away from the tower and the point where, to the observers in normal time, he had disappeared, Hook stripped off his clothes. He kept his old black boots on. Now he could really move. Friction would have flamed his blue coveralls in no time; the Boosting process gave his skin perfect immunity.

He pelted down the hillside and he kept a close lookout for the Boosted Man. No ordinary, slow time mortal might be able to see a man running in speed time; but another Boosted Man could. If Hook was spotted the Boosted Man would fry him, at once, without thought. The Novamen normally sent one or two of themselves to a planet to sort trouble. Hook did not yet know just what the dossier on him looked like; but the Boosted Men must by now have such a dossier. And a Novaman thought faster than most computers—as fast as Hook was thinking now.

The party from the tanker had entered a building where no doubt payments and loadings were being discussed. Hook leaped the perimeter wire fence, going over it in one bound, feeling the power in the wires as he passed, knowing they were sure death to any flesh and blood of normal origin. He didn't much fancy what that current would do to his organo-metal skin, either.

To his vision everywhere on the field, in the park, over by the loading bays, activity had ceased. Men were in the act of work, and appeared frozen, stiff. Hook whistled past them in fast time and headed for a bay where cans were stacked. The cans looked interesting, marked with flowery descriptive phrases, each can a full hectoliter. They were surprisingly

118

light. Hook hefted one from the back of the stack, where its absence would not immediately be seen, balanced it by its yoke sling over his shoulders, and sprinted back for the fence, took off in a long leap, hit running and burned the grass back to the tower.

When he set the can down he saw why it was light. Set in a recessed bottom the tiny anti-grav unit functioned when the can was lifted, all twenty-two gallons of it. Hook set it down, anti-grav device undermost, as the red arrows indicated, right by the foot of the ladder. Sharon would see it. Hook stepped back. Well, he just hoped she made it out.

Now he must see about the Boosted Man.

The dis gel gun electro surgically plugged to his wrist was not a Delling. Hook quite liked Dellings. It was not a Parkat, either. What its origins were, Hook was not completely sure. He'd taken it from the corpse of a Boosted Man. The important thing about the wrist gun was that it withstood the friction of fast time movement. Hook nipped across to Rhus, whose pose remained by less than a millimeter what it had been when Hook passed this way before, and searched the Krifman's pockets for the dis-gel gun's magazine. He yanked it out, careful not to scorch the cloth of the pocket, slapped it back into the gun.

His own clothes were pretty shabby by now. He took the weapons belt and the Martian Mega and bundled them up into the small of his back where the friction wouldn't melt them, tied the belt and took off. Over the fence once more and with a running dive he could head for the fancy hotel. If the Boosted Man happened to glance out of the window of the loading shed he would see the field with the people at work at the tankers in the park; and he would also see a naked man hurtling along in speed time. Hook sweated it out and whistled into the front entrance of the hotel. The place was swank—very Top-Star swank indeed.

There was no percentage here in slugging someone who

vaguely resembled him, getting cosmetics from the store here and disguising himself. Whoever he chose would be known and would have acquaintances here, even friends. Hook, by force of circumstances, must remain a loner.

That suited him fine.

Ninety-nine per cent of the plans the poor old dynaman Selkas had dreamed up for Duke Everest had been instantly jettisoned. RCI had brought him here. Once the Boosted Men, in the guise of loners or of RCI, came on the scene, they became the prime target.

Still in fast time Hook raced down to the loading bays. He took some care to keep as much as possible out of direct line of sight of the windows where the Boosted Man might casually glance out. Once inside bay number three he could forget the precaution; the Novaman was in bay number one. Hook peered over the frozen shoulders of the handlers, checking the ledgers and the output terminals. The computer, obviously, was not here. Its location might give a useful clue to the whereabouts of the headquarters of the Shylao. Hook spent a heartbeat in running down the latest arrival. Working a fresh name into the register earlier on called for a spot of cunning contrivance; but Hook was a jack of all trades—with the familiar proviso that if you then call him a master of none you made what might easily be a fatal error—and by rerunning tapes, punching out a false time of arrival slot and patching it in, he convinced the computer log that a Taynor Ken Zero had been all duly logged down for a hectoliter can of The Virility Gene that morning. Whether or not the main computer would accept it remained to be seen. Hook felt it would; he'd had the beast on line and his instructions were coded subtly enough so that his EAS instructor might have been pleased. Correction. There had been no pleasing Captain Carpenter. The man had been as much a machine as his beloved computers. On a whim, and because it amused him, Hook punched out, after the name Zero, "Capt. Retd."

Now he could finish the job at the hotel.

He booked Zero in as from that morning and then hunted up a smart set of plate-fab clothes from the storerooms at the rear of the hotel tailors. He chose a mid-gray tunic and trousers, with a yellow line over the shoulders and arms and down the sides of tunic and pants. It was a smart rig, no doubt about it. He took also the matching gloves and hat with moveable visor, which he hung on his belt. These clothes would not burn up in moderate fast time.

Around him everyone in the hotel was held in the stasis of slowtime—which was normal time. Hook took a breath. He selected an alcove in the coffee room, all shiny imitation walnut plastic and synthipersian rugs, carried a drink across and sat down.

He switched to normal time.

Instantly the room came alive. Men were laughing and talking and drinking. Some were discussing deals. The atmosphere was so odd to a loner like Hook he felt he must still be dreaming in speed time. Hotels of this nature existed all over the habited portions of the galaxy, of course; but they were patronized by people with credit cards. Hook doubted if there were more than half a dozen cards in the coffee room. These loners had come here to buy The Virility Gene. They were well treated during their stay by the Shylao. No wonder the whole affair was so beautifully organized. Hook doubted if there was another comparable place in what he knew of the galaxy. Loners—acting out the fantasy of being of the assured of the galaxy, with wrist credit cards! Amazing.

There were some weird customers among them, too. Real hard cases, roughnecks of the galaxy, acting like upper-bracket econorg execs. Hook felt his amusement as a live and enjoyable bubble.

He was soon engaged in conversation by a welpac who showed radiation scars on his face he hadn't bothered to have plasticed. Everyone tried to buy as much of The Virility

Gene as they could afford. Hectoliter cans were the favorite. The few tankers going out were run by self-help groups of people without wrist credit cards. They were embryo econorgs themselves, little groups of people who had got together and tried to stand against the might of the conglomerates.

"I'll clear enough to settle down out of this little lot," confided the welpac. "This is my second trip. First time around I was jumped by hijackers."

"My sympathy," said Hook, smoothly. "It's hard enough to make a living without those vermin."

"I do agree, taynor—?"

"Zero. Got in this morning."

A fight broke out over by the bar. Old habits died hard, even in the luxury provided by the Shylao for their guests. The welpac frowned and dusted down his tail.

No alarm raised outside, so Hook could only hope that Sharon had got clear. That included the curd Rhus, too, for if he went under he'd drag Sharon with him. What explanation, he wondered, would they have for the can of The Virility Gene? They'd know what it was, all right, from the flowery descriptions on the can.

If Sharon didn't get out, it wouldn't be Hook's fault. He'd done what he could for her. Her back-up team would extricate her and Rhus. Maybe next time they'd try through the front door, legitimately, like these people about him now. Trouble was, the galaxy was such a big place you might never meet the right contact. The Shylao didn't care. They could entertain these buyers here in this luxury hotel, prefabricated just for the period, and at the same time they could allow those destitute no-hopers to die slowly alongside the road to the spaceport in the town where Hook had made planetfall. It all added up; but it added up to a picture that did not please Ryder Hook.

If you had the money to buy Vilgene, you were all IQ. If

you could find the right contact, that was. Those poor devils who believed Vilgene was to be found at the cross on some faked treasure map paid, also; it was their misfortune, as it had been Brett's, that they hadn't met the right contacts.

The whirlpool of stars was so big, you could drive yourself silly just thinking about it.

And the Shylao protected their headquarters. Carshder proved that.

After they'd caught him and dealt with him, they'd brought him back to Wearyville and dumped him back where he had arranged to meet Selkas. A chilling warning. And the Shylao also did not wish to deal with the econorgs. That made sense. These loners down here would pay the prices asked, for they knew they could sell Vilgene at a hundred times what they had paid for it. The conglomerates would soon force the buying price down. That was their style.

Hook had not forgotten Michael Michael when he and the girl and the Boosted Man walked in for coffee.

Back on Sykoris, where he'd had his last bust with the Novamen, Hook had not looked like Hook. Michael Michael did not know what he looked like. And if Hook acted true to form then Michael Michael would never be able to use any information he picked up down here on Shyle. You had to fight fire with fire.

Michael Michael was laughing. "A good day's work, sir, most encouraging." He was a tough bastard, a Homo sap, neatly dressed in a business suit, with a shock of dark hair and a ruthless flare to his nostrils and a meanness about the lines set at the angles of his mouth. But beside the Novaman he looked like a mewling infant. Hook's attention centered on the Boosted Man. Big and strong, of course. A fine head with a neatly combed mass of blond hair, perfectly turned out, of course. Expensive clothes, of course. Manicured hands, of course. A powerful, rugged, experienced face, of course—with that magical hint of nobility the Novamen could always give themselves. Of course. Of course Ryder Hook would fry him at the first opportunity.

And then Hook looked at the girl.

Ryder Hook did not believe in love at first sight. He did believe in something very like it, though. He felt the jolt go through him, a physical pain, a blow to the heart, a breathtaking blow to the solar plexus. His guts ached. It was not that she was incredibly lovely, with her features not quite perfect and yet sensually alive and lovely because of that. It was not that her figure made him react like a goaded stallion. It was not that the violet of her eyes surveyed the room with an amused appreciation of the foibles of human nature. It was none of these things, and yet it was all of them combined—and much more.

Hook wanted her.

She laughed and Hook knew what spine-tingling fingers was all about. If a man has never experienced that sensation, then he cannot comment on it. Hook knew about it, now.

"Oh, Michael—it's not all work today, is it?"

Her voice—superb! What she said meant nothing for the moment beside her voice. Hook had to force himself to sit and clutch his cup with its revolting mess of coffee. He knew he was staring. By Dirty Bertie Bashti's odiferous pants! If he didn't break this spell, the Boosted Man would glance over and Hook would be remarked upon. He had to get himself under control.

"You feel all right, Taynor Zero?"

Hook rejoined suffering humanity.

"Perfectly, thank you." He found he could manage a dazzling smile for the puzzled welpac. "If you'll excuse me."

There were plenty of other females in the hotel, delightful creatures from all the races represented here, and Hook knew why they had been brought by the buyers of The Virility Gene.

He felt a sudden physical coldness. Had this girl whose name he did not know and yet whom he knew he had known for years, whom he would know for the rest of his life—had she been brought for the same reason? And—*by a Boosted Man*?

Michael Michael was speaking with the utmost deference to the Novaman. He called him sir all the time, occasionally slipping in, with great daring, A Taynor Fenshaw. So the bastard's name was Fenshaw. Hook walked casually out of the coffee room and his mind seemed even to him to be a seething cauldron, spilling over, blinding him, making his face feel hot and his limbs ache and his guts rumble, all in sympathy. Fenshaw. And Michael Michael. And that superb girl . . .

He went off to loading bay number one, walking along normally, observing the activity. From what he saw and by the way the incoming tanker line ended, he surmised the operations would be over by nightfall. He went into bay number one and speeded up into fast time and whistled into the office. He went to work goaded by a black and savage anger.

Taynor Fenshaw's name and Michael Michael's name were expunged from the records. He had the computer on line and ticking over, flicking in and out of speed time and no doubt causing a considerable confusion to the operators. But he was past caring now. He knew he ought to take it easy, as he had when he fed in Ken Zero; but he could not control himself. For Ryder Hook, that was a cardinal sin.

When he had finished monkeying with the records he went out, slipped back to normal time and sauntered along to the flier park. To saunter at all was agony; but he had to get himself back under control, and so he made himself stroll along without a care in the world. This world, this world of Shyle. He had uncounted cares on other worlds of the galaxy. They meant nothing now. The loading bay office had

125

contained no information on the girl. He checked over the fliers, mentally marking up those worth stealing, and went back to the hotel. The Boosted Man and Michael Michael were still in the coffee room, drinking spirits, laughing. The girl sat at a small side table, nursing a soft drink, studying a small red notebook. Hook eyed her as long as he dared and then took himself off to the hotel booking office.

He checked out the reservations.

Fenshaw... Michael Michael...

Tayniss Iola Gervase...

Iola...

He remained there a long time, long enough for one of the serving robots to move a tentacle a good centimeter. He roused himself. Iola... He had to get her out of the clutches of the Boosted Man, that was imperative. Fenshaw could not be allowed to carry out what he so obviously intended. Iola...

If the arrival of the Novaman Fenshaw had made Hook change his intentions and forget about the dynaman Selkas, then his discovery of Tayniss Iola Gervase had in its turn driven all thought of anything but her out of his head. He had seen enough of her, even in this short space, to know she was desperately unhappy. She laughed with a gay brittleness that pained Hook. Back in the coffee room he saw the trio about to leave, and he heard the way the Boosted Man talked to Michael Michael, all brusque authority and dark power, and he saw how Iola so quickly moved out in the lead to avoid the inevitable unpleasantness from Fenshaw. Poor kid! She must lead one hell of a life. Well, all that would end. Ryder Hook would take care of her from now on, even if they rowed enormously and fell out and hurt each other. Hook's experience of that kind of human relationship was so limited as to be no guide; but he would learn. It would be marvellous, learning with Iola Gervase.

The sun, that old F-type Jarhed, had sunk by now. A very great deal had happened, so considered Hook, meaning just one thing, since they'd spotted the watch tower. This morning he hadn't known Iola Gervase existed. This night she was the motive for his actions. And what a lumpen fool he was! But he wouldn't have it any other way.

The Shylao were packing up now, making the last business deals, all the incoming tankers empty and ready to take off, the customers ready to tuck into the last lavish dinner and then depart in their own transport.

For the dinner which was something of an occasion, a celebration of a successful business venture, the guests were seated according to a rota read out by the chief robot waiter. The names were called. The guests went in, laughing, happy, to take their seats. The dining room blazed with lights, the tables were marvels of napery and silver and glass. Everything was done in style. Most of the guests had turned out in style, also; but there was still the occasional old loner who'd never had a wrist credit card and who dressed as he pleased. A mal in a pair of old denims walked past Hook, and a sap with an oily set of metal-fab clothes wandered in. Hook felt he looked passable enough in his new mid-gray tunic and trousers with the yellow stripes.

This might be a formal dinner; everyone wore their guns.

Old habits died hard.

Hook's quirkish addition of "Capt. Retd." after the name Zero in the register bore strange fruit now. Groups of people went in as their names were called, sitting where indicated. The laughter rose on the scented air. This was a time of jollity and pleasure, of good companionship and the drinking of wine, of friendship. Hook marked Iola and her two companions. He moved out of their sight beyond an artificial flower spray, speeded up, sizzled across to the robot, snatched the list, did a quick oblit-spray job on his name and

127

on the name of Michael Michael, wrote them in again in a perfect forgery of the computer print-out typeface, transposed them.

He whistled back to his flower spray and walked out on the other side, in slow time, composed, smoothing his yellow-striped trouser leg. No one could have blinked an eye in the time he had been gone.

The robot bellowed the names.

"Taynor Argant Del. Tayniss Lorna Fernal."

Two people seated themselves and the robots pushed their gilt-encrusted plastic chairs in comfortably. The tables blazed with candlelight, the napery sparkling, the silver mellow.

"Taynor Holt Fenshaw. Tayniss Iola Gervase."

Hook watched them, his eyes burning. He took a hitch to his tunic, smoothing it. The flowers exuded perfumes.

"Captain Ken Zero. Tayniss Rhylla Halmar."

He walked toward the table, toward his chair. A woman walked at his side, a Shashmeeri, voluptuously sensual in the Shashmeeri fashion. Hook did not look at her. He kept his face blank, his hands loose; he could feel the sweat in his palms. With motions like those of a rusty robot he pulled the Shashmeeri woman's chair out for her; a robot would push it in when she was seated. Hook couldn't have said what she was wearing. He took the back of his own chair. He looked down at Iola Gervase.

She wore a white gown so that her skin glowed golden and smooth, so lovely Hook wanted to touch it, to stroke it, to feel its softness. Her hair fell to her shoulders, a rich brown, like his own brown hair, and the lights of the dining room caught in her hair and sparkled like fireflies. Her violet eyes looked up in surprise as Fenshaw half-rose.

"What happened to Michael?"

Hook ignored him. He looked down at Iola Gervase.

"I am honored, Tayniss Gervase."

He pulled the chair out decisively, and sat almost before the robot could push the chair in.

Iola looked him in the eyes and Hook saw the shock there, the reflection of his own bewilderment, his own loss of identity, his own helplessness.

"Captain Zero," said Iola Gervase. "I—I did not expect—"

"Neither did I."

They stared at each other like lost souls.

"The pleasure is mine, Captain Zero," said Iola Gervase, and the color rose soft and lovely into her cheeks.

12

He awoke to the sound of a tin whistle.

Holt Fenshaw, Boosted Man, devil, stook looking across Iola Gervase, his face hot and ugly.

"What happened to Michael? Who's this clown?"

"Sit down!" yelled a La'chorite from across the table, his eating utensils already in his grip pouch. "Who's it matter who's where at a time like this?"

The man blowing the tin whistle tooted a trill and then a cadanza, shrilling the piercing notes through the hot and happy atmosphere.

Hook had not—could not—take his eyes away from Iola Gervase. She looked back at him. Each knew the other was drowning in the other's eyes. No incongruity could touch Hook then, no fashionable cynicism of romantic tomfollery. He was making a complete idiot of himself, so all right, then! Romance would still exist in the Whirlpool of Stars, and no blasé has-beens who had run through their expectancy of sexual life could with all the mockery of which they were capable alter that one jot or tittle. It was very pleasing to be contemptuous of old roués who, when their powers waned, became converted and started in preaching to youngsters that they mustn't. All Ryder Hook knew as he sat next to Iola Gervase and fell into an easy conversation with her, all he wanted as they chatted and laughed and the dinner party boomed and roared on all about them, was that this should go on for ever.

They talked. They talked of inconsequential things, and he learned little enough about her and he understood the reasons for that, the same reasons as she could learn little about him. But personal histories meant little, too. They discovered each other. The living breathing human beings they were, at this moment, were what mattered. They made contact on an immediate and human level of happiness and laughter and joy.

The Shashmeeri girl on Hook's other side, provided by the management, perforce must seek conversation with her other neighbor. The woman buyer, most charming and refined, next to whom Hook should have been sitting was deep in conversation with Michael Michael. Fenshaw, having accepted a puzzling mistake, tried to get into the conversation. Each time he spoke Iola jerked, and a muscle quivered in her cheek, and she turned to him with a smile forced through her involuntary tensing up; but she made some polite non committal reply and then turned back to Hook.

Hook felt there was no need to question her about her relationship with Fenshaw. She did admit, however, that she worked as his personal assistant, and they were with RCI, and that she had been born on Earth, and she wasn't sure if she liked her job or not; but that she had great plans. Then they talked about all the other wonderful things in the galaxy that did not have to do with work and econorgs and loners and The Virility Gene. Hook could talk charmingly when he wanted to; he did not wish to now. He spoke sincerely, and he knew Iola spoke in the same way. The dinner passed in a dazzlement of mutual wonder and enjoyment.

News passed down that two guards had been found shot in a watch tower, and for a space reality obtruded, then they could go back to discussing just what it was about the music of Jernitz that so uplifted the spirit, why tea was so superior to coffee, whether the novels of Charles Greyson should be linked in a semantic series or treated as independent texts, if the fate of that unfortunate Gholan system could have been averted if the Gholanese had trusted a divine spirit instead of shamans. The time passed very swiftly, and the brandy was served and people were yelling and screeching and the time for the orgy approached.

"I've absolutely no idea what I've eaten, Captain Zero."

"Neither have I, Tayniss Iola. I do not think I have ever—" There was no need for him to finish that.

Her violet eyes reassured him she felt exactly the same.

Ryder Hook's preoccupation with Iola Gervase was not one hundred per cent complete—oh, the missing portion of his attention was minute, minute!—but he still retained enough of his old self to know the forensic sniffers would have been at work around the watch tower; once the forensic boys put a kit together and fed it into the machinery they could pick up his own body emissions as a match against one of the three at the watch tower. He filed that away in his mind and knew it made no difference. He'd have to be dragged away kicking before he'd give up a second of time with Iola Gervase.

The maddeningly exciting pulses from Fenshaw's Boosted body reached Hook through the intervening body of Iola. Hook had never experienced such an intensity of the process before nor had he felt that near superhuman lifting of his abilities in quite this quality before; somehow there was a subtle and distinct difference in experience with this Boosted Man.

Probably, he thought, gloating, that was because he'd never experienced it before with Iola at his side.

Down at the far end the table and chairs had been removed by the robots, couches had been wheeled out and already men and women were sampling minute drops of The Virility Gene and were hard at work. A buyer had to test his wares, didn't he?

People around Hook and Iola rose as the robots came for the chairs. Michael Michael wandered up with the charming lady buyer, and he winked at Iola. She let him have a tiny half-smile. Hook's face remained blank. He was introduced as Captain Zero and he found he could smile as though in greeting when in actuality he smiled at the fatuousness of where that idle addition of "Capt. Retd." had placed him.

No one thought to question where his commission had originated; the ironical thing was that he could have substantiated it. He had served as Captain of a cruiser— quite legitimately—during one of his escapades a few years back. That had been a relatively happy time, too. Now they all took drinks and wandered down to watch this new set of fun and games.

Hook stood right next to Fenshaw, the Boosted Man.

"Are you going to test your purchase, Taynor Fenshaw?"

"I expect so, Captain Zero." Fenshaw spoke as though addressing some mud worm in a dirt hole.

Hook turned away at a touch on his arm. The Shashmeeri girl stood there smiling provocatively at him.

Hook bent to whisper in her ear.

"There's a bonus in it for you if you occupy Holt Fenshaw."

She arched her eyebrows. Then she giggled.

"I'll always go for a bonus, honey. I'll occupy him good!"

"That's a girl." Then, in his new expansive, silly mood, Hook added: "And you look charming, my dear, positively radiant."

She simpered and, thus primed, went to work on Fenshaw. Hook put a hand on Iola's arm. The touch set him afire with naked lust, and he had to force himself to calm down. This was no ordinary business. This was the business of his life so far.

To a Novaman, as far as Hook knew, one girl was as good as another, and a Shashmerri was always something special. Hook and Iola were able to drift away from the main party where the orgy was now hotting up. They walked together, close together, down toward the opposite end of the long room, talking.

"You're pulling out as soon as this is over, Iola?"

"Yes. There is business. Always there is business. Holt Fenshaw is a most powerful man with RCI. I know."

"My partner is going somewhere I've no wish to go. Is there a chance you'd find a seat for me?"

She smiled at him. Her smile would have destroyed him had his business not already been done.

"I can't, Zero! I can't. It's—it's something you wouldn't understand."

This was a shadow between them.

Hook could not say: "Oh, yes, Iola, I understand. Your boss is a Novaman. Even you don't know the whole of it."

So, instead, he said: "But I want to see you again."

"I do, too! But..."

"Well, then?"

Her smooth forehead showed the faintest indentation above her adorable nose. "There are things I can't explain. Oh I wish I could—but I cannot. I am not—I am not permitted—"

"Most of the people here are loners, without allegiances to econorgs, Iola. You do have that loyalty. I understand that."

"That is part of it. You could—"

What would be the best way of explaining that her boss was a blight in the galaxy and that he was going to be destroyed just as soon as Hook contrived it? That probably wouldn't go down well. Not well at all. But it was true.

Once Fenshaw was out of the way, and Michael Michael, too, Iola could be freed. It would be not simple. It would be direct.

The morality of it made absolute sense to Hook.

"I know you don't like working for Fenshaw—"

"No! But I have to. I have my orders, my duty—it is not easy..." She squeezed his arm. "I believe I shall be promoted soon, and then I'll have my own department. I can say goodbye to Holt Fenshaw then."

Hook kept his face straight. If Ryder Hook had anything to do with it, Iola would say goodbye to Fenshaw much quicker than she expected.

He stopped by a damak-velour couch. He did not release his hold upon Iola. She stood looking up at him, her eyes meeting his, her breath soft and sweet. Slowly, feeling the magnitude of the occasion, Hook bent. He kissed her. He kissed her and he felt the fires flickering all along his limbs and devouring his body. She responded. She was the flame. He held her to him and put a hand on her white gown and she put her slender hand on his and pressed. He could feel her heart beating. She moaned and her lips grew hot and soft under his.

When they pulled apart Hook couldn't say anything.

Iola said: "We shall be leaving soon. I'd like to know you before then, for there is something—something I can't explain." And her violet eyes clouded. "I never thought I could—it is unbelievable—I had always imagined it would have to be someone like Holt Fenshaw. But now—I really do think—"

Hook kissed her again. She put his hand on her breast and he could feel her heart beating like a promise of soft winds, and the dawn, and sunshine, and the pulse of life, and all the silly things a man thinks of at times like these.

"I have two tablets of Vilgene—we ought to—"

"That won't be necessary, Iola."

135

"I know that! But it would be—would be—"

So there, on the damak-velour couch they slipped the tablets of Vilgene into their mouths, and they made love and for Hook there had never been anything remotely like it in all his experience. It went on and on and the experience grew and grew. He remembered every little detail, and yet all was overlaid with that silly romantic rosy haze that would in normal times have revolted him as sentimental nonsense. He knew that this was not sentimental, it was not nonsense—it was really happening and it was tremendous. And then came the final realization that he didn't give a damn if it was sentimental and it was nonsense. That made no difference. No difference at all.

He'd begun this latest series of adventures as Abel Klark. Then he'd been Duke Everest. Now he was Captain Zero. And Cap Zero had come about only through a quirk, a strange chance. He felt deep regret that Iola did not know him under his real name. But he retained shreds enough of sanity to refrain from telling her he was really Ryder Hook. She worked for a Boosted Man—although not for much longer, not much longer!—and a word out of place and exit Ryder Hook from the Whirlpool of Stars.

The orgy was winding down and many people had already left by the time they came down out of their universe of passion back to the mundane world of Shyle. Hook felt wonderful. Iola looked radiant. At the other end of the room Michael Michael and the Shashmeeri woman were still hard at it. Holt Fenshaw had taken over another partner. Everyone looked wild. But the room was emptying. It depended on the amount of The Virility Gene they had taken. Hook and Iola looked at the others without envy. Arms about each other's waists they moved down to rejoin the party. Hook felt light, insubstantial, rejuvenated, his eyes opened to the possibility of a new life, a life he had never dreamed could be his.

"If you think I'm going to forget you, Iola—if you think I'm going to let you go—"

"I have to go! You don't understand—and I cannot explain."

"Maybe I know more—" He stopped. After Fenshaw was out of the way. Then would be the time.

"You can't know what I'm talking about. No one does. Even to hint that there is anything to know is dangerous—"

"There are very many dangers in the galaxy, Iola."

"Look, Zero. I have to go back to Thalius. We have a major agency there."

"I know it. Pleasant little world, not unlike Earth."

"Yes, I have to go. Once I get my promotion, then I will be freer, having my own department."

"I'll wait," said Ryder Hook. "I'll wait. But don't be surprised if I drop in on you on Thalius—"

"You mustn't! You daren't!"

He knew what she meant. The Novamen would not take kindly to a stranger, and a loner at that, chatting up—as they would phrase it—one of their employees. The Novamen used people. They had a mass army of zombies, they had the Doorn, in their agencies scattered among the stars they employed millions of different people who worked for RCI and had not the slightest idea they worked for the Boosted Men. But Ryder Hook wouldn't let that stop him. It never had before.

He smiled at Iola. "And if I say I'd dare anything for you, that would sound empty boasting, a love-sick idiot's bleating!"

"Oh, no. Not you!"

A thought occurred to Hook that had been driven out of his infatuated brain along with just about everything else. Yes, he ought to get back to the welpac Brett and fill him in on what had been happening, and that would not be for the dynaman Selkas's sake, either. But both those two were unimportant. His time would soon be up in which he had allowed himself a little relaxation before he checked up on Shaeel and Karg. He would have to go see what those two clunkheads had been up to. So he could with extreme reluctance let Iola go back to her foul agency on Thalius. Once he had seen to Shaeel and Karg he could space out to Thalius, and then—and then no damned econorg and especially one run by the Novamen would stop him.

"You're leaving right away? Back to Thalius?"

Iola hesitated. Hook did not miss that. Then, and he guessed with certainty out of concern for him, she lied.

"Yes. To Thalius, straight away."

He found it interesting that he could tell she lied so easily. Yet he loved her for that attempt to shield him. Of course, the Boosted Man was here to do just what Hook was here to do, and that was follow the Shylao and find out the secret of Vilgene. Well, if Hook had to go after the damned Virility Gene in order to stick with Iola, that was what he would do.

Michael Michael and Fenshaw were making pigs of themselves. As Hook and Iola approached Michael reared up, flushed, sweaty, still massive. He pushed the Shashmeeri woman away. He stared all flushed and furiously at Iola.

"Where've you been, Iola? You know I wanted you!"

He started towards them and Hook let his reflexes take over. He would have to handle this just right. Fenshaw had stood up and was looking at the scene with an indolent and amused interest. If Hook flipped into speed time the Novaman would instantly react.

"Get out of my way, gonil!" said Michael Michael. Hook recalled what had happened to this man in *Vandeneuf*. The shattered wrist had been healed without a mark. He did not move.

"I do not think Tayniss Iola wishes to see you."

Michael Michael's face showed the shock of that. He lashed out at once. Hook caught the wrist—it was the same one—he felt the dis-gel gun there, he bent the wrist back and again that wrist shattered so that pink bone showed through.

Michael Michael screamed. Hook pushed him away, still screaming, holding his wrist. A gun appeared in Holt Fenshaw's right hand, pointing at Hook. It was a Tonota Eighty and it could punch him, Iola, the whole dining room into slaked embers. In the next instant . . . Iola stood in front of Hook. She stood tall and beautiful and absolutely stunning to Hook in his besotted state.

"No, Holt! Not Captain Zero!"

"Why not? Is he so special—a curd of a Homo sap? No one breaks the wrist of any of my people and gets away with it. Stand aside, Iola!"

Whether he would have shot or not, Hook did not then know. He felt that a Novaman wouldn't give a tuppenny damn about a personal assistant. He'd shoot and hire a new girl. Iola stood braced, completely committed. Hook prepared to tense his muscles to shoot the dis-gel gun. If he gave a thought that he would be firing from behind a woman's skirts he knew that as the woman was Iola the situation was admissible.

Fenshaw stood for a moment, waiting for Iola to move.

Iola said: "I'll make up for it, Holt. I promise. But you mustn't harm the Captain."

"You're giving me orders!"

"No—I'm asking—"

Hook said, loudly: "I'll apologize to Michael Michael, and I'll pay for his hospitalization. I think we all lost our tempers."

"That's no damned good, gonil—"

A voice lifted from the end of the room.

"Michael Michael and Holt Fenshaw!"

"Here comes the local Shyle security goons," said Hook, speaking quickly. "Now we want no trouble with them at this late stage, do we?"

Holt Fenshaw's gun vanished. He looked as mean as a man might well look. Hook hadn't missed that slip, when he'd referred to Hook as a curd of a Homo sap. The man had once been of Homo sapiens stock himself, before he'd gone through the RCI Powerman Project and been turned into a Boosted Man. Now Fenshaw gestured to Iola.

"I'll overlook it this time, Iola. Take Michael to medical and have him seen to."

Iola flashed Hook a glance and he saw all the relief there in her violet eyes. He nodded.

"I'll settle the bill."

Fenshaw licked his lips. "You'll settle the bill all right, Captain Zero."

Iola took Michael Michael away. Hook watched them leave by the far door as the security men tramped down the room.

The guns in their fists did not allow any argument.

The leader, Colonel Roote, chief of the Shyle security services at this interface, waved his gun at Hook. Hook decided that if the ident-kits had sniffed him out he would have to do something very special, some nasty Hook ploy; but—

"Stand aside, please, Captain Zero."

Colonel Roote swung to glare at Fenshaw. "You call yourself Holt Fenshaw? You have been very foolish."

Hook stood next to a thick-lipped goon in tight uniform, whose Tonota forty was lined up on Fenshaw's midriff and whose metal-fab clothes, too tight, creaked. His jaws kept rotating as he chewed stim-gum. He looked no more moronic than he had to be to hold down his job.

"What the hell are you talking about, Colonel?"

All the arrogance, all the naked display of superiority, habitual to a Boosted Man flashed evilly from Fenshaw. Colonel Roote was taken aback; but he growled his words and now he took a joy from what he was saying, what he was doing.

"Foolish, I said. You may have registered into the hotel but you did not bother to register for Vilgene supply. Your tanker has been loaded; but you have no right, no order, nothing. We do not like people who steal from us, Fenshaw."

Fenshaw looked astonished.

"We registered for our supplies—"

"Save it for the Shylao! Now hand me your Tonota and be very careful when you uncouple your sleeve gun—I wouldn't want to fry you unless I had to."

With a dozen guns centered on him there was only one thing a Boosted Man would do.

Fenshaw speeded into fast time.

To the others he would have vanished.

To Hook, who also speeded into fast time, the Boosted Man appeared as a man moving at a normal speed, and the onlookers froze into their unnatural positions of apparent stasis. Here was an interesting phenomenon of the Novaman's mentality. Fenshaw could simply have run from the dining room. He could have got clear away, as far as he knew, for in his view no one could stop him...

Instead, and with an evil look of pure enjoyment he lugged out his gun. He was going to blast them all before he took off. He was going to leave his visiting card, the certain sure sign of the Novaman—death!

The enforcer at Hook's side, stilled in mid-chew with the tip of his tongue wedged between his lips where he was in the act of licking the trickle of juice down his bristly chin, partially masked Hook from Fenshaw's eyes. In speed time Hook put out his hand without moving his body. The strange fact struck him that Fenshaw moved comparatively slowly. Now that was odd. Hook had been so struck by the enormous vitality of the Boosted impulses that had set his own body tingling. He had never before encountered such power, such force. And yet Fenshaw's speed time came nowhere near matching Hook's.

Fenshaw just managed to draw his Tonota and aim it.

Then Hook pressed the goon's forefinger against the trigger of his gun and the blast lashed out and chopped away Fenshaw from throat to knees. The remains toppled.

Now Hook would experience those horrible symptoms of withdrawal. Now the Boosted Man was dead all those marvellous powers would die with him. Once again Hook would become a mere normal mortal, a member of humanity...

He almost retched with the vile hunger in him for those wonderful powers to continue...

He was in normal time again, and Fenshaw's head and legs were bouncing on the floor, and the goon was licking his stim-gum juice and beginning to look surprised. Colonel Roote opened his mouth to bellow, and Hook shouted first: "Well done! Very well done! Colonel Roote, you must be very proud to have such smart men serving under you. That curd Fenshaw's gun came out with speed—very very fast indeed!"

Well, they could all see the fire-warped gun, thrown across the room. Fenshaw had drawn and thought to beat them.

Colonel Roote looked at his man. "I'm surprised, Corporal, but you thought fast. Well done." He started shouting orders. He sent his men off running. To Hook, he said: "I must apologize for an unpleasant scene, Captain Zero. But we get hijackers and gonils trying to steal the Vilgene from the Shylao. From time to time. We deal with 'em, though. They don't fool us."

"You are to be congratulated, Colonel."

Hook was taking no notice of what the Colonel said, what he said in reply. His Boosted powers had not died with Fenshaw. He felt them pulsing and coruscating through his body. He was still a Boosted Man, and the Boosted Man who had resonated his capacities lay dead. A great joy and a great dread filled Hook. Had he, at last, become a fully Boosted

142

Man? And would he now allow those dark mechanical forces that had overwhelmed the Boosted Men to destroy him, also?"

He shuddered there as they swept up what was left of Holt Fenshaw.

Then the truth hit Hook.

There must be another Boosted Man here, somewhere. A Boosted Man sent in as a back-up probably hiding out, ready to come streaking in in fast time and sort out this situation. The heady imaginings of a moment ago passed. He was still a mortal human being, speeded into Boosted status only when another Boosted Man was nearby.

He could have shouted for joy.

He could have wept for grief.

There were still all the things to do he had decided on. Everything fitted together, here, all the parts of the whole falling together into one picture. He would do the job and then go to Thalius. He would not again give up Iola Gervase.

With that lure, that enticement, that enormous extra reason for living, Ryder Hook felt capable of surmounting all the obstacles confronting him. Sort out poor old Brett, find out about Shaeel and Karg—and then hightail it for Thalius and Iola. Yes.

That subtle difference of emphasis, of center, of quality about this Boosted Man's resonances continued. Fenshaw, it was now clear, had been a lower-grade Boosted Man, sent in as the front man. The more powerful of the two had waited to observe and he it would be who was to follow the Shylao. Hook could not quite clearly sense the direction of the Boosted Man. If the bastard came in now, to check up on Fenshaw, Hook would have to deal with him, and do it damn quick, too.

The trick with the loading bay number one's register had worked. Hook did not wish to wear out his welcome here, despite that he had a kind of in with Colonel Roote. He

143

would conclude the deal he had been working out with that welpac and cadge a lift back; the story about his partner pulling out would work there. Or he could simply steal a flier. Either way, he'd keep an observation both on the Boosted Man and the Shylao.

Yes, the whole whirling gaggle of stars seemed very good to Ryder Hook as he went through either to wish Michael Michael well or to punch him on the nose. He'd say goodby to Iola for only a short time and then they'd meet up on Thalius. Then . . . !

He went out of the door and crossed a plastic apron to reach the medical center. The Boosted Man, Hook sensed, was hanging about over there. He didn't want to have to go out after the gonil; but if he had to he would. He saw Iola walk out of the medical center and he shouted and waved. She saw him and waved back.

"Michael Michael's been taken to our tanker. He won't make trouble for you. I heard about Holt." Well, the Colonel's men had been after Michael Michael. It looked as though Iola was trying to get the curd away in one piece.

"What happened to the enforcers, Iola?"

She made a gesture, walking up to him, so lithe, so beautifully formed, slender and curved, so gorgeous with all the passions they could arouse together, her wide violet eyes warm and soft upon him. "They let him go. But—we must now say goodbye—"

And Ryder Hook understood.

He didn't believe it, of course, not right then; but he understood, and he saw the depths of his own folly.

"I don't want to say goodbye, Iola. Not now."

His fist rested on the butt of the Martian Mega. He knew what he should do.

"It won't be for long! Now poor Holt is dead it looks as though I've got my promotion early. I'll be stepping into his shoes now. It's going to be wonderful when you get to Thalius—but I cannot take you with me now."

"No, Iola, of course not."

A shout broke from overhead and the tanker floated there, an anti-grav scoop waiting to whisk Iola up and away.

She leaned forward and kissed him. With a savagery that made her gasp Hook seized her and crushed her to him, bruised her lips with his, sought to drag her into his very being.

"Hey! It's not the end of the world! We've only just met— and yet we've known each other for years! But I must go, now—darling Zero—I'll see you soon."

She broke from his arms and turned. She walked quite slowly back to the anti-grav scoop. She did not look back, and Hook felt the black relief of that.

He actually took out the Martian Mega and held it in his fist, the barrel pointing at the ground.

He ought to, of course. He had sworn to do this, had he not? If any curd in the tanker yelled he'd flame him without a second thought.

Iola Gervase reached the anti-grav scoop.

Hook looked after her.

The scoop whisked up and vanished into the belly of the tanker. In the last instant, as the riding lights shone upon the scoop, Iola leaned out and waved.

And Ryder Hook waved back.

He should have shot her.

Of course he should.

Hadn't he sworn to destroy the power of every single Boosted Man he met?

But Iola was a Boosted Woman.

Should that have made any difference?

Should it?

The tanker whisked up and the first rays of that old F-type

Jarhed shone upon its swollen flanks. It turned and raced away into the dawn.

Hook looked at the gun in his fist. Hand-in-hands into the sunset had never been his game. Iola Gervase, Boosted Girl.

Ryder Hook knew he'd only just started this game—and it was likely to be the game of his life.

IT'S ALWAYS ACTION WITH

BLADE

HEROIC FANTASY SERIES

by Jeffrey Lord

The continuing saga of a modern man's exploits in the hitherto uncharted realm of worlds beyond our knowledge. Richard Blade is everyman and at the same time, a mighty and intrepid warrior. In the best tradition of America's most popular fictional heroes—giants such as Tarzan, Doc Savage and Conan—

		Title	Book #	Price
———	# 1	THE BRONZE AXE	P201	$ .95
———	# 2	THE JADE WARRIOR	P202	$ .95
———	# 3	JEWEL OF THARN	P203	$ .95
———	# 4	SLAVE OF SARMA	P204	$ .95
———	# 5	LIBERATOR OF JEDD	P205	$ .95
———	# 6	MONSTER OF THE MAZE	P206	$ .95
———	# 7	PEARL OF PATMOS	P767	$1.25
———	# 8	UNDYING WORLD	P208	$ .95
———	# 9	KINGDOM OF ROYTH	P295	$ .95
———	#10	ICE DRAGON	P768	$1.25
———	#11	DIMENSION OF DREAMS	P474	$1.25
———	#12	KING OF ZUNGA	P523	$1.25
———	#13	THE GOLDEN STEED	P559	$1.25
———	#14	THE TEMPLES OF AYOCAN	P623	$1.25
———	#15	THE TOWERS OF MELNON	P688	$1.25

AND MORE TO COME . . .

TO ORDER

Please check the space next to the book/s you want, send this order form together with your check or money order, include the price of the book/s and 25¢ for handling and mailing to:

PINNACLE BOOKS, INC. / P.O. Box 4347
Grand Central Station / New York, N.Y. 10017

☐ CHECK HERE IF YOU WANT A FREE CATALOG

I have enclosed $_____check_____or money order_____
as payment in full. No C.O.D.'s

Name_____

Address_____

City_____State_____Zip_____
(Please allow time for delivery)

INTRODUCING TWO NEW, EXCITING, ACTION-PACKED ADVENTURE SERIES OF SPECIAL INTEREST TO KUNG-FU FANS

Meet Sloane

Eastern martial arts and the raw violence of the American West join in the most dynamic Kung-Fu Western Series ever written.

Sloane #1:
THE MAN WITH THE IRON FISTS
by Steve Lee $1.25

Sloane—the toughest, deadliest, Kung-Fu warrior of the Old West in a no-holds-barred, electrifying new series of violence and adventure.

Sloane #2:
A FISTFUL OF HATE
by Steve Lee $1.25

Flying fists and lethal feet match themselves against blazing guns as Sloane rips a bloody path through Western trails.

Meet John Crown

A fast moving blend of cops and Kung-Fu in the exotic setting of modern Hong Kong.

Crown #1:
THE SWEET AND SOUR KILL
by Terry Harknett $1.25

Hong Kong—city of sins, slums, and splendor. John Crown—hard-drinking, hard-loving, hard-fighting and the toughest cop in the Far East.

PINNACLE BOOKS PRESENTS
THE TWO ACTION-PACKED BEST-SELLING
WESTERN SERIES WRITTEN FOR
TODAY'S TOUGHEST FANS!

Read one—you'll want to read them all.

EDGE by George G. Gilman
Edge is a new and different western series, his blade is indestructible . . . and Josiah Hedges is the most violent hero to ride out of the old WEST!

_____	P596	THE LONER #1	1.25
_____	P703	TEN GRAND #2	1.25
_____	P667	APACHE DEATH #3	1.25
_____	P597	KILLER'S BREED #4	1.25
_____	P590	BLOOD ON SILVER #5	1.25
_____	P668	RED RIVER #6	1.25
_____	P599	CALIFORNIA KILL #7	1.25
_____	P265	HELL'S SEVEN #8	.95
_____	P704	BLOODY SUMMER #9	1.25
_____	P333	BLACK VENGEANCE #10	.95
_____	P600	SIOUX UPRISING #11	1.25
_____	P669	DEATH'S BOUNTY #12	1.25
_____	P560	THE HATED #13	1.25
_____	P624	TIGER'S GOLD #14	1.25
_____	P672	PARADISE LOSES #15	1.25
_____	P727	THE FINAL SHOT #16	1.25

ANGEL by Frederick H. Christian
Angel, the toughest lawman in the West. In Record Group 60 of the National Archives in Washington, D.C. there is abundant documentary evidence to the effect that for a number of years the Department of Justice employed a special investigator named Frank Angel who was directly responsible to the attorney general of the United States.

_____	P613	FIND ANGEL #1	.95
_____	P614	KILL ANGEL #2	.95
_____	P615	SEND ANGEL #3	.95
_____	P452	TRAP ANGEL #4	.95
_____	P501	FRAME ANGEL #5	.95
_____	P584	HANG ANGEL #6	.95
_____	P643	HUNT ANGEL #7	.95

If you can't find any of these titles at your local bookstore, simply send the cover price plus 25¢ for shipping and handling to: PINNACLE BOOKS, 275 Madison Avenue, New York, N.Y. 10016.

ALL NEW DYNAMITE SERIES

THE DESTROYER

by Richard Sapir & Warren Murphy

CURE, the world's most secret crime-fighting organization
created the perfect weapon — Remo Williams — man pro-
grammed to become a cold, calculating death machine.
The super man of the 70's!

Order		Title	Book No.	Price
_____	# 1	Created, The Destroyer	P361	$1.25
_____	# 2	Death Check	P362	$1.25
_____	# 3	Chinese Puzzle	P363	$1.25
_____	# 4	Mafia Fix	P364	$1.25
_____	# 5	Dr. Quake	P365	$1.25
_____	# 6	Death Therapy	P366	$1.25
_____	# 7	Union Bust	P367	$1.25
_____	# 8	Summit Chase	P368	$1.25
_____	# 9	Murder's Shield	P369	$1.25
_____	#10	Terror Squad	P370	$1.25
_____	#11	Kill or Cure	P371	$1.25
_____	#12	Slave Safari	P372	$1.25
_____	#13	Acid Rock	P373	$1.25
_____	#14	Judgment Day	P303	$1.25
_____	#15	Murder Ward	P331	$1.25
_____	#16	Oil Slick	P418	$1.25
_____	#17	Last War Dance	P435	$1.25
_____	#18	Funny Money	P538	$1.25
_____	#19	Holy Terror	P640	$1.25

and more to come . . .